# KNIGHT
## OF
# Birmingham

*Book 8 of the Knights of the Castle Series*

*Lori Hays and
MarZe Scott*

Macro Publishing Group
Chicago, Illinois

This is a work of fiction. Names, characters, places, and incidents are products of the author's imagination or are used fictitiously and are not to be construed as real. Any resemblance to actual events, locales, organizations, or persons, living or dead, is entirely coincidental.

*Knight of Birmingham* by Lori Hays and MarZé Scott © Copyright 2020

Macro Publishing Group
1507 E. 53rd Street, #858
Chicago, IL 60615

ISBN eBook— 978-1-952871-06-1



Cover designed by: J.L. Woodson www.jlwoodson.com
Interior design by: Lissa Woodson www.naleighnakai.com
Cover image: Woodson Creative Studio www.woodsoncreativestudio.com
Editors- Naleighna Kai and Brynn Weimer
Contributors- Stephanie Freeman, Naleighna Kai
Beta readers- Kelsie Maxwell, Debra J. Mitchell, Karen D. Bradley, Anita Roseboro-Wade, and April Bubb.

# KNIGHT

## OF

# Birmingham

*Book 8 of the Knights of the Castle Series*

*Lori Hays and
MarZe Scott*

*Lori Hays*

*This book is dedicated to my friend C.T. and all the women who are unjustly serving time. Though she is away from her family, she keeps going strong by working, reading Christian books and learning to crochet. She keeps in touch with her two young children and family who are taking good care of them, until they can be safely back in her arms. I am so proud of your strength and perseverance in the face of adversity. You are going to do amazing things when you are safely back home.*

*MarZé Scott*

*This book is dedicated to my father, Carl Bruce "Sonny" Carter, a complicated man with a good heart. Your love of creativity will forever live within me.*

# ♦ ACKNOWLEDGEMENTS ♦

Lori

I have so much gratitude for my husband, kids and friends who listened to me whine as I learned the complexities of becoming an author, supported me and sacrificed time with me while I hid away in the writing cave.

I would like to thank Naleighna Kai's Tribe Called Success. Especially our fearless leader Lissa Woodson (Naleighna Kai) and MarZé Scott. Thank you to Lissa for inviting me to be a part of your tribe and recognizing me as someone who could write a book. And for putting up with my insecurities through the process and teaching me so much in such a little time. And huge thanks to MarZé Scott for being willing to jump in immediately when I needed help, guiding me through the process, and agreeing to co-author my first novel with me. Without these two amazing women, Knight of Birmingham may never have happened.

Thank you to J. L. Woodson, cover designer extraordinaire. Thank you for to all the tribe members, editors, and beta readers who immediately answered the call when we were racing to the finish-line.

MarZe Scott

I thank God for all things, but especially for the gifts and talents placed within me and the friendships they have fostered. Without God, none of what I do would have purpose, nor would it be possible.

Thank you to my family, The Royals. You all give me life every day. To my bonus Prince, Fredrick L. Griffin—I will always remember your quiet spirit and heart of gold. Your hugs were the best. "You don't have to explain what's already known" is what you always said. I know you loved us. Gone too soon, but I thank God for each day you were a part of our lives. Fly High, Young Prince.

Thank you to my siblings, Cecil and Tamika—you both keep me motivated to chase my dreams and that money.

Thank you to Rochelle Smith for checking on me—"I just wanted to hear your voice and know that you're okay." Indeed, I'm okay.

To my big sister, my Butter Bean, Kim Steed—I wonder why it took so long for us to find each other? Most people find their best friends in their childhood, but we had to wait because the world wasn't ready for us. Thank you for riding this rollercoaster called Life with me. Thank you for imparting your wisdom and love, for teaching me to set boundaries and to be brave for myself, for drying my tears and making me talk when I wanted to shut down, and for the shenanigans and laughter. Because of you, I'm a better person.

To Portia Mann—Thank you for being my spiritual mother and for creating a space where I could work in my gifts and walk in my purpose. I love our relationship. One day, you'll give a sermon on what we talk about word for word and what a day that will be!

I'm eternally grateful for my literary family, my Tribe. You all light up my literary life. Thank you, Fairy Godmother, J.L. Campbell—You have been a great encouragement in my journey. You inspire me to write more and to be accountable to my process. London St. Charles, my cheerleader and writing buddy—Thank you for keeping me motivated about my writing when I felt like giving up. Thank you Shakir Rashaan for being my big brother (even though I'm older than you) and an ear to listen. Your weekly check-ins always came right on time. I always learn something about freedom when we talk. Thank you to my new literary sister, Stephanie M. Freeman. We both love to write and crochet, but the way you write a love scene gives me tingles. Teach me your ways! To my bestie, Shannan Harper, the calm to my ratchet—Thank you for making me laugh when I wanted to cry and for your love when the Pretty Lady was down. You'll never know how much your gifts mean to me.

Thank you to J.L. Woodson, graphic designer extraordinaire—your talent never ceases to amaze me. Your covers are absolute fire! Thank you to the beta readers: Anita Roseboro-Wade, Kelsie Maxwell, Brynn Weimer, Karen Bradley, April Bubb, and Deb Mitchell. Your keen eyes and love for reading make every story I write better and better.

A special Thank you to my literary sister, Lori Hays, for entrusting me to bring magic to your words. I have had a great time getting to know you. I look forward to working with you more.

To my Tribe Chief, friend, and literary mom, Naleighna Kai—God knew what He was doing when the Universe brought you my way. You've nurtured me in this journey, especially when it got hard. I appreciate the love and attention you've given me.

Thank you to my reviewers—your voice is appreciated.

To anyone else who I didn't mention, charge it to my head and not my heart as I love you all more than words could ever express.

# Chapter 1

*9:30PM, Saturday, March 3rd*
*Nadaum*
*Middle East*


*"Where am I?"*

The last thing Candace Simmons remembered was sitting at the table in the cafeteria of the Faith Rescue Mission. She was sharing lunch with other volunteers after a morning spent fulfilling their community service requirements at a center in Birmingham, Alabama.

"Why is it so dark?"

Candace opened her eyes, her heart raced, thinking she was dreaming. She peered around the blackened area. Her head pounded as if her brain were trying to escape her skull. Echoes of moans sent chills up her spine. The stench of mildew caused her stomach to twist. Metal dragged on concrete as she lifted her hands in front of her face. She felt the warmth of her breath on her moist skin, but still couldn't see. Heavy bands of cold slid down her arms causing tremors to course through her body.

"Where am I?" a young woman's voice cried out.

"What the hell is going on?" another female spoke.

Candace's eyes stung as a bright light flooded the dark space and a garage door rolled up followed by a chorus of women screaming.

"Welcome home, my treasures," a man with a thick accent greeted, his smooth tenor tone far too inviting for the occasion. "You are going to serve a great purpose. Get these women to my wives and begin the process," he called out over his shoulder.

A group of men wearing white robes and headpieces filed in, pulling the women up, some by their hair, others their arms. Candace watched in horror as the men yanked cloth bags over the women's heads, laughing at their screams, cries, and protests.

"Somebody help me," she screamed just before her hair was yanked from behind. The world went completely dark.

# Chapter 2

*12:00 PM, Tuesday, March 3rd*
*Birmingham, Alabama*

"What do you mean she's not here?" Meghan asked, trying to remain calm with the woman at the front desk of one of the transitional homes sponsored by her non-profit. "It's Tuesday and that means family day. She should be here. Where is she?"

The woman behind the desk, Layne Phillips, according to the nameplate on her desk, pushed her glasses up on her nose, and heaved a sigh as the line of visitors behind Meghan increased.

"There is no one here by that name," Layne answered in a thick Southern drawl. "Now, please move along so I can get the rest of these folks checked in."

Meghan shook her head. "That can't be right. I was just here last week. I walked in the courtyard with her." Scanning the lobby, Meghan was met with hard glares and furrowed eyebrows. One woman sucked her teeth as she folded her arms under her breasts. Turning back to the blonde receptionist, Meghan implored, "She's supposed to be here for another six months. She's violating parole if she leaves, and she would never go back to prison intentionally. I need to speak to the house manager."

Layne flipped her golden tresses off her shoulder. "You're looking at her, ma'am." Layne stood and extended her hand to shake Meghan's.

Meghan glanced down at the woman's manicured hand, then back up to the single raised eyebrow without accepting her hospitality.

"I started on Sunday after the previous manager and her staff didn't show up to work," Layne explained, her smug attitude evidenced by the caustic tone. "Luis Fry appointed me. Now, please leave before I call someone to have you removed. The other families have been waiting patiently to see *their* loved ones while *you* stand here being rude."

Meghan narrowed her gaze on Layne, taking note as the woman pursed her pink lips to one side of her heavily powdered face.

Layne put a hand on the telephone and leered at Meghan as if she dared her to stand at the desk one second longer.

Turning on her heels, Meghan breezed by the families who stood between the desk and the front door. Arriving at her Toyota Highlander, she pulled a cell from her briefcase. She entered a number and waited for someone to answer. "Hello, thank you for calling The Journey Beyond," a warm mature voice answered.

"Hi, can I speak to Jill Maynard?"

"I'm sorry, no one by that name works here. Is there anyone else you'd like to speak to?"

"No, thank you." Meghan disconnected the call, her heart rate increasing and her hands trembling as she proceeded to make another call. And yet another. All of the staff Meghan had painstakingly hired for the three houses The Journey Beyond sponsored were replaced without her knowledge. Her agreement with the Department of Corrections allowed them to run the day-to-day operations of the houses was so she and her staff could focus on the rehabilitation of clients. Now, the people she knew and trusted had been exchanged for individuals with which she had no history and without warning. Not one of them was vetted and none of her people called to ask her about the sudden change. Meghan tapped a phone number with her thumb.

"Good afternoon, Mr. Fry's office," a raspy voice greeted on the opposite end. "How may I help you?"

"Hi Mae. It's Meghan. Is Luis available?"

"One moment."

Meghan twirled a coppery loc around a finger as she listened to the classical harpsichord recording that played while she waited. Luis Fry's name coming up as part of the issue, certainly raised an eyebrow. They had been able to keep their personal issues out of their professional lives so far, but their interactions had been tense recently since they'd been forced to work together as part of a government initiative.

"Luis Fry speaking." His voice boomed like a radio announcer's and just as commanding. One of the reasons Meghan fell for him before she knew who he really was.

"Is there a reason I wasn't informed of the staffing changes that have been made at the transitional houses?" she asked, trying to rein in her anger. "According to our contract, I'm to be kept in the loop about all personnel in order to protect the women housed there."

Luis laughed, and the sound was hollow and dark as he taunted, "Well, it seems there's a lot you don't know, Ms. Turner. You'll need to call the District Attorney and see how these modifications further affect you."

"Aren't you supposed to be my sponsor? Or my investor?" Meghan snapped, as she looked out the window of her vehicle, watching a young family walk by, the smallest toddling after a puppy. "Didn't I sign a five-year agreement with you? I mean, my name *is* still on the website as the founder."

"Call Willingham," Luis insisted, ignoring her assertions. "He's pulling the strings on this project."

Luis was right, District Attorney Scott Willingham had drafted and filed a new contract that limited her access to The Journey Beyond transitional homes. She had full access to staff and financial records when she entered the agreement four years prior. Meghan was confused how she would have missed the memo that her rights to know who was being hired and fired had been taken. She didn't receive a notice to appear in court, but it was possible she overlooked it as she focused on the influx of applications for potential clients. At any rate, DA Willingham seemed to have an axe to grind and had it aimed at her efforts on several occasions and now Luis has joined him.

The Journey Beyond was a nonprofit organization that worked with women who found themselves on the ugly side of the law. The focus of the program was to get them out of prisons, and in some cases into the transitional group homes sponsored by the non-profit. This put them on track to be reunited with their children and prepared them for a successful life outside of concrete walls and metal bars.

Meghan was just starting out and had depleted her funds buying the properties and hiring the necessary staff. Luis helped her secure the contract with the DOC which paid for keeping the homes open, but Meghan couldn't be involved. Only twelve months left in the contract and The Journey Beyond would resume full responsibility of the homes. It couldn't happen soon enough.

# Chapter 3

Durabia was a not-so-distant memory for Rory as his flight landed at Birmingham-Shuttlesworth Airport. He wound his way through Terminal A and customs on the ground floor, then stepped outside the automatic doors and breathed in the warm Southern air.

"Malakai," Rory said, excited to see his brother who he hadn't laid eyes on for the six months he'd been out of the country on business.

Malakai had parked the BMW 8-series in the "no stopping" area of the passenger pick-up like he was president of the company. He popped the trunk so Rory could load the titanium Samsonite luggage and slid his sculpted frame from behind the wheel, wrapping Rory in his arms before giving him a kiss on each cheek.

Rory squeezed Malakai and moved out of his confining hold.

"It's so good to see you but, damn bro, how do you travel twenty hours across the globe, stopping in a few different cities and still smell like you just got out of the shower."

Rory patted Malakai on the back, giving him a once-over. "First class has its advantages."

Malakai laughed and Rory shook his head before getting in the driver's side of his car and closing the door before Malakai could protest.

Malakai, the younger of the two, stomped his foot like a petulant child, sighing heavily as he slid into the passenger side.

"It's good to see you too, Malakai," Rory beamed, a bright smile splitting his face despite his fatigue. "I've missed you. You good? How about Mom and Tarah?" Rory shared his estate with his family and his staff, but his mother and sister were more likely to be waiting for him to walk through the door.

"Yes, all is well," Malakai assured, glancing at his brother. "They're looking forward to seeing you for brunch tomorrow." He reached to turn the volume down. "My question is, why didn't you take the private jet? You would've been here hours ago. Didn't you say that guy had money?"

Rory rubbed his forehead and chuckled as he drove past the Southern Museum of Flight, then took the looped entrance to Interstate 20 West. "Yes, but I haven't gotten used to all of that fanfare. I haven't quite settled into the whole 'knighthood' of it all."

"If you can't, I will," said Malakai.

"There's a lot that comes with this position," Rory explained. "Lots of important people I'm connected to. I'm working on being the best man for the job, but it takes some adjustments when it comes to balancing things with my purpose. So, I adjusted from economy to first class."

"That's a start," Malakai shrugged. "I definitely know what to do with that kind of money. I think that whole Knight thing should have skipped you and come to me," he said, and Rory thought a thread of jealousy had crept into his brother's voice. Surprising, especially since the Knight's main purpose was purely humanitarian and addressing the issues that world governments had swept aside. Malakai could care less about anything except himself.

On a personal level, Rory's efforts in the Middle East had cost him a position in The Castle when Khalil brought together his former students to deal with the predicaments that plagued the place he founded. Unfortunately, in Rory's involvement in the underground safety network Khalil established years ago, he couldn't leave the Middle East at that time as it would put many lives at risk.

The shelters he built in several Middle Eastern countries, served as both a cover and safe haven and would have met the ire of the people who had the power to shatter his entire operation if they understood how far-reaching the organization had become. Instead, he was given the immediate status of being a Knight and was now being brought back to deal with a problem that was closer to home. El Zalaam had been shut down in Durabia, and the Kings had taken down another sex trafficking ring and organ harvesting pipeline. Yet somehow a new one popped up with an indirect link into his hometown.

"It's not about money," Rory explained, getting annoyed with his brother's greed and ignorance. "The Kings of The Castle are responsible for the universal community. We create opportunities for improvements in our local jurisdictions and around the globe. The change the world sees, starts with us."

Rory always made sure his brother and the rest of his family were well taken care of. Khalil and the Kings provided awesome opportunities, but it was Rory who sought to expand beyond what he'd been given. His brother always found ways to squander any fortune that came his way. This resulted in Rory putting the brakes on any free money, so Malakai now had to earn anything that landed in his bank accounts.

Malakai's silence caused Rory to glance over to find him snoring. "Just like the old days," he said before rubbing his arm to avoid startling him. "The roar of a motor still puts you out after a few minutes on the road."

"What, what's going on … Rory?" Malakai questioned, rubbing his eyes to clear his vision and yawning wide enough to suck up every available ounce of oxygen in the car.

"I've been gone for half a year and you fall asleep in two seconds." Rory laughed despite the twinge of concern for his brother's fatigue. "What's up? Why are you so tired anyway? What have you been up to?"

"Man, Fry's party last night was lit," Malakai explained, looking out the window at the passing semi-trucks. "I'm getting too old to play so hard, I guess."

"Didn't I warn you about him?" Rory said with a sigh, gripping the steering wheel, his knuckles turning red from the tension.

"Luis is harmless," Malakai said with a laugh. "Just because you have an issue with him, doesn't mean I have to. He hasn't done anything to me."

"So you're willing to wait for him to cross you or worse, before you leave him alone? Give it time. You'll learn."

Malakai waved off his brother's warning and adjusted in his seat looking out of the window, keeping his focus on the passing scenery.

Rory drove through the gates of his estate and parked in front of the water fountain instead of pulling into one of the stalls. He didn't want to wake his friends who managed the household and other properties in exchange for an equitable salary.

The attempt to allow his friends to sleep in was unsuccessful. Either that, or they hadn't been to bed yet. He walked into a warm welcome from James, Marcus, Neveah, and Izzy. The kids were asleep even with all of the celebrating going on.

"Brother," Marcus exclaimed, embracing Rory and patting his back three times before releasing him. "It's so good to see you. We've missed you around here. We have a lot to catch up on, bro."

Rory stepped back and took in the sight of his friends standing in the grand pavilion.

"Where's my mother?" James frowned, glancing over his shoulder at Malaki. "He didn't tell you?" Rory shook his head. "She's in the city with my wife's family. We just lost an aunt. She'll be coming back in a couple of days."

"See, brother. If you had been on that private jet—"

"Save it," Rory snapped, disappointed that his brother chose to be petty. They could have easily detoured through the city before making it home.

His mother had redecorated for the spring season. The ornamental pillars in each corner of the space held new floral arrangements of aromatic white lilies and purple hydrangeas artistically arranged in her favorite marble vases that Rory gifted her after his first trip to Durabia. Through the arched doorway just past the grand entrance to the pavilion, his friends had his favorite Clase Azul Reposado tequila waiting along with a spread of meats, cheeses, nuts, and dried fruit on the buffet in the dining room.

"We thought you might like some refreshments to hold you over after your long day of travel," Neveah said in a sleepy voice. She was beaming with the glow of pregnancy, despite her obvious fatigue.

"Thank you, Neveah," Rory said, bringing her into a brotherly embrace. "It's so great to see you."

Nevaeh yawned. "Gloria just went down, so I was up, anyway. But you're right, I have to sleep when I can," she said while rubbing her growing baby bump. "See you in the morning." Nevaeh shuffled to the suite she shared with her husband, James, and their two children in the East wing.

"The rest of you, too," Rory declared as he walked towards the remaining group, giving them each a warm hug before sending them off to follow Neveah. "I can't wait to catch up tomorrow. Thank you for everything. I'll see you in the morning."

Rory settled in a comfortable seat at the table once he had the room to himself. He poured a shot of tequila and ate some dried apricots as he pulled out his phone. Notifications from various news sites he followed lit up the screen—a severe weather warning, several new Instagram followers, and a unexpected text from Luis Fry inviting him to a charity gala being held by an organization supported by the Kings of the Castle to raise awareness of human trafficking.

Dwayne Harper, King of Lawndale, had texted that there was something going on in Birmingham and that he should be aware. Luis Fry's name came up, along with some other Alabama politicians. Luis a white-collar defense attorney turned state prosecutor, represented the upper echelon of the political world. A number of them, along with Luis, had been to Durabia recently, then slid into Nadaum, landing on the Castle's radar.

Rory had established several women's shelters in honor of his Mother while in Durabia. He was a special ops officer as part of an underground safety network that spanned several Middle Eastern countries. He hadn't been involved in the expansion projects and missions of The Castle, but he knew that wouldn't last long. Especially, since recent issues seemed to connect Nadaum, Durabia, and Birmingham somehow.

# Chapter 4

Meghan walked into her office at Journey Beyond—or JB as everyone called it, located next to Birmingham City Hall across from the popular Linn Park. The Jefferson County Courthouse was a brisk walk through the grassy area. She spent a great deal of time there working on client cases.

Thoughts of how she made it to this place raced through her mind. A series of unfortunate life events led Meghan to Andrea Phelps and Theresa Stevens, or Mama Ann and Mama Tee as the neighborhood folks called them. They took her in after her mother, Jackie, committed suicide a few weeks before she graduated grammar school.

So many relatives had come out of the woodwork to take care of Meghan, but quickly readjusted their position when they learned that Jackie's best friends had been named executors of the estate. Her father's life insurance and the proceeds from the sale of her childhood home were put into a trust and had been enough to pay for college and law school, leaving a little bit of a nest egg to keep her comfortable. This came in handy when Mama Ann, Jackie's best friend, and Mama Tee, Ann's life partner, invited her to stay with them. Even when Meghan became of age to take care of herself, she stayed with her mamas and contributed to the household by stocking the cabinets with groceries so she wouldn't become a financial burden.

*"I know we can't take the place of your parents, especially your mother," Mama Tee explained, wrapping twelve-year-old Meghan in her arms, a wayward tear falling from her warm brown eyes. "I'm hoping we can at least ease your pain with a lot of love and some of your mother's favorite carrot cake when the occasion calls for it."*

*"Can the occasion be every Saturday?" Meghan whimpered, holding onto the memory of the quiet Saturday mornings with cake and coffee she had with her mother. "At least for a little while?"*

*"Sho'nuff, Sweetnin'," Mama Tee assured her, brushing a loose copper curl away from Meghan's eye. "We can do that."*

Mama Ann and Mama Tee made sure that Meghan was always surrounded by their children, nieces and nephews, and whoever else on the street needed extra affection. This was the family she came to know and love as she finished high school, obtained her undergraduate degree from the University of Birmingham, and law degree from Cumberland School of Law at Samford University.

Life with her newfound "relatives" was very different than it had been when she lived with her mother in one of the most affluent areas of Birmingham. She felt and looked out of place with her alabaster skin, red hair, and piercing blue eyes that were a stark reminder of the man who now resided with the angels. Before moving in with Mama Ann and Mama Tee, she couldn't have imagined leaving the luxury of her four-bedroom home in McCalla, a distance down the highway from one of the most unsafe cities in Alabama.

Where she lived in Bessemer, the closest well-stocked grocery store was five miles away. Public transportation was the only way to get to school since most centers of learning on their side of town had been closed due to lack of funding. Abandoned buildings in the area were easy targets for gangs to use for sex trafficking or drug dens. Law enforcement wasn't to be trusted. Street justice was rampant in the town where the odds of becoming a victim to street violence was one in twenty-six. Safe was a four-letter word matched by another word—pray.

Despite the high crime rate in the area and danger just a stone's throw away, a prevailing sense of community was alive. Neighbors were more like extended family. The men built homemade games and swing sets in the yards so the kids could play in a safe place. Bell peppers, yellow squash, and onions grew in abundance in the community garden where they worked together with other block clubs to nourish each other with fresh and healthy foods.

For years, Mama Ann and Mama Tee were the subject of whispers amongst the neighbors and kinfolk, as well as the topic of many Sunday morning sermons. All because the two women lived openly, lovingly, and happily in a racist and homophobic Alabama. However, once someone was invited over for a meal of fried fish and grits or smoked turkey and greens, they'd sooner argue that Santa Claus existed than be concerned about what the two women did behind their closed doors. Mama Ann and Mama Tee loved everyone, and they were repaid in kind for the love they showed.

One of the desires of Meghan's heart was to show them how much she loved them too. The Journey Beyond was her attempt at keeping that promise.

# Chapter 5

Meghan slumped into the wide leather chair behind her hand-me-down oak desk, pulling her red hair into a messy bun. She straightened the white shirt that clung to her curves from the thin sheen of perspiration that formed during the walk to her office. Mascara streaked her flushed cheeks from the tears she had finally allowed to come on her drive back from the group home. Meghan couldn't remember a time when she felt so defeated. Exhaustion was an understatement.

"What in the hell happened to you?" Sally questioned, her pronounced Southern accent nodded to her roots in Eastaboga, Alabama. "You could've been run over by a truck by the looks of you."

Sally Decker, her partner, had a history with the Alabama corrections system after serving time for stealing food from the corner store when a three-year relationship with her girlfriend came to an end and left her destitute. Making matters worse, when the clerk tried to stop her, she gave him a right hook that landed him on the ground. The concussion he received from the fall, and the argument with law enforcement, got her a broken collar bone and sealed a five-year sentence. Every board review extended her time as punishment for protecting other cellmates from the abuse and violence inflicted by guards and prison residents. That's why Meghan knew she'd be perfect for The Journey Beyond. Even though getting to the silver haired woman took a little convincing.

* * *

*"Excuse me Ma'am? Ms. Decker?" Meghan was almost jogging to keep up with the woman as they left the auditorium of the Hyatt Center where the Annual Social Work Conference was being held. She nearly tripped, trying to pull a business card from her portfolio. "I'm Meghan Turner with The Journey Beyond, and I just wanted to say how much I loved your session."*

*Sally kept walking, ignoring Meghan for some unknown reason.*

*"I'm looking for people to join my team, and I think you'd be great," Meghan explained, panting as she chased the woman. She had underestimated the fact that a woman who was heavy-set and easily old enough to be her mother could move like a track star. "I'm sure you're busy. Would you mind slowing down a little. I feel like I'm racing in a fifty-yard dash."*

*Sally stopped suddenly, and Meghan almost ran her over. "Meghan is it?" she asked, leveling a hard, steel gray gaze on her. "Look, I'm not looking to get involved with anything right now. So, just keep on going, young lady. You're barking up the wrong tree."*

*Meghan sighed, trying to ascertain where the woman's animosity was coming from. "Please, if you'd just give me a minute, I'd like to tell you about my organization. Then I'll give you my card and leave you alone."*

*Sally glanced at her smart watch, tapped the screen, and started a timer. "You have fifty-seven seconds left, better be quick."*

*A smile spread across Meghan's face as heat rushed to her ears. "My goal is to create a safe place and resource for young mothers of color, Black and Brown women when they leave the system. But first I have to get them out of the system by shining a light on the fact that their sentences were unfairly administered. Here's my card. Please call if you want to know more." Meghan extended her hand, placing the card in Sally's palm as the alarm on her stopwatch chimed.*

*Sally tapped it to turn off, tucked the card in her pocket, and walked away without another word.*

*Meghan assumed she'd never hear from her again. She was surprised a few weeks later when she saw her in the audience of a seminar Meghan was giving at First Christian Church of Birmingham.*

*"I think I like what your program is about, Miss Turner," Sally declared, the corners of her thin lips turning up, softening her masculine features. "When can we start working together?"*

*"Please ... call me Meghan. How about tomorrow?"*

* * *

"She's gone, Sally," Meghan sobbed as she propped her elbows on her partner's desk. "Candace is missing from the group home. No sign of her. I don't know what to do. She's so close to getting the girls back."

Sally banged her fist onto her desk. "Shit," she exclaimed as she stomped the floor, the buckle of her green canvas army boots jingling. "I should've talked to you about this sooner, but I wanted to put the pieces together."

Meghan sat up to put her focus on Sally.

"There have been several women who have gone missing from the system. I've been trying to figure out what's going on since some of my clients weren't showing up to court for their scheduled appearances. Same thing with Maria."

Sally shoved the sleeves of her green and black flannel shirt up her arms, dug into a file cabinet, extracted a stack of manila folders, and handed them to Meghan, who blinked to clear her vision and get a handle on this new development.

"All of these women are missing," she said, and there was a sadness in her tone that sent a spike of fear in Meghan's heart. "All of them are our clients. All of them are young, Black and Brown single mothers who've lost their parental rights and didn't have a lot of family. Most of them are missing from Tutwiler. Two of them from other JB Homes. I was going to talk to you about it today." She tapped the top folder in Meghan's hands "I would've never thought Candace would be one of them. She doesn't fit the profile. Her skin is darker than the other women and she still has her rights."

Meghan's eyes grew wide, taking in the thickness of the files in Sally's grip.

"How long has this been going on? You can't keep this kind of information from me," Meghan yelled, dropping the folders on Sally's desk, before pacing the office as she pulled out her phone. "Where is Maria? We need to get the Sheriff and DA involved. I'm going to set up a meeting."

She had two partners, Sally, and Maria Sanchez. Sally was familiar with prison life from the inside. Maria's mother and sister were currently serving lengthy sentences in Tutwiler due to the fact that they killed her father while in the act of raping Maria. It wasn't the first time he had done so, but he threatened to kill her sister if Maria ever said a word.

The challenges of that came along with their efforts at JB, meant more tears than any one person should have to shed. Every day they received calls from family members who had a niece, daughter, cousin, mother, sister, or girlfriend thrown into jail for a year or more on trivial charges like possessing a dime bag of marijuana, drinking in public, or stealing food because a dire hunger left them little choices. Some were more serious charges, like assault or attempted murder, but nine times out of ten the victim was the woman's abuser.

Meghan, Sally, and Maria each had twenty cases and a waitlist of over 250 women requesting their services. They were now looking to hire more staff for their ever-growing program. Meghan had raised some funds with the help of a few well-connected individuals and was awaiting approval for a number of grants she had applied for. Being a white woman in Alabama usually had its perks, but advocating for single women of color who were marginalized had placed her at the bottom of a mountain of red tape and bureaucracy.

Black and brown people raising their voices against the many transgressions and atrocities committed against them had been woven in the fabric of American society for centuries. When a White person like Meghan chimed in, they were met with disdain from their family, friends, and peers who felt the way things worked was just fine. She was also faced with distrust from the very people she aimed to help, because they had no reason to believe she was genuine. Until she proved otherwise.

Now, in addition to navigating this new political landscape and growing social unrest, another thing had been added to the list of things she didn't have time for—missing women directly related to her organization.

# Chapter 6

"You are worthless," said the man with a deeply accented voice Candace remembered from the training sessions with the "wives" in the mansion where the women were kept. "I don't know what they thought I could do with you. You don't listen, you're nowhere near as beautiful as the other women. What a waste of flesh."

The room where she was forced to sleep on the floor with only the white robe she was given to cover her nakedness was dim and clammy. She couldn't make out his face through the rough material of the sack pulled over her head. She was jerked roughly to her feet as they yanked her out of the room.

"Where are you taking me?" Candace cried.

No one answered.

She couldn't see, but it felt like they walked a quarter of a mile before her hands were tied behind her back with what felt like rope. She was pushed ahead a few more steps.

"Yes boss, she is here. We will take her to guest house number seven." the man with the deep voice chuckled.

Candace shivered in the dark, stuffy vehicle that smelled of manure. She was thankful for the sack on her head which probably made the smell more tolerable. She bounced around as the vehicle drove, her empty stomach doing somersaults.

*I'm glad I haven't eaten the food they provided, or this would be a lot worse.*

The vehicle slowed and Candace could hear beeping noises from the front window, then the clang of a gate opening up before they started moving again.

"Get her," the deep voice said again.

The door opened and she was yanked out by her left arm and tossed to the ground. The sandy feel under her feet was so hot that it burned her skin. "This cloth is too good for you." The deep voice that Candace was beginning to resent, said with a hint of pleasure in his voice.

The man pulled her to her feet and ripped the robe off and tossed it aside. She shivered at the loss of the thin barrier as he stroked his hand over her buttocks and said, "But her body is lush. We might have other uses for her before her fate is decided." Another set of arms caught her before she landed on the ground again.

"Put her in the takhzin in the courtyard behind the house," the deep voice said to whoever caught Candace.

This man had soft hands and was gentler in the way he handled her. He didn't speak as he guided an exhausted and humiliated Candace through a door into a room. He closed the door behind him before removing the covering from her head.

It took a minute to adjust to the light after being kept in the dark for so long. She blinked several times before looking up at the man who seemed to be showing some kindness after all the other men handled her like the worthless piece of flesh they claimed she was.

"The things Akbar said about you are untrue. What is your name?" The man wearing tan cotton pants and a matching cotton tunic said, making sure to only look in her eyes.

"Candace" she said, her voice dry and raspy. "Where am I? What is going on?".

"You are in one of the many houses of Futtaim, the man who procured you and the other women. I cannot provide you with any of the details from their end, only my part in a larger scheme of things. I am Emir, a security guard, but I am not with the men who put you here," he explained to Candace, continuing to maintain eye contact. Not once did his gaze lower to her naked body. She wasn't sure if it was because he was being honorable or if he felt the same as the other men. "I am going to share something with you for your own comfort. If this is known to the other men, I will be killed."

"Then why tell me such a thing?"

"Because we only have a short time and I need you to trust me."

Candace held in her reply, aiming to listen to whatever he had to say. Maybe something he mentioned could help her escape.

"I work for the Sheikh of Durabia," he confessed. "I will get you out of here. We do not treat women like this where I come from." He closed his eyes and lowered his head as if the admission weighed heavily on him. Candace realized she was completely naked in front of this man and recognized the fact that Emir did not look anywhere else but her eyes.

"I need you to keep your wits and strength about you," he warned. "Do not fall into despair. When it is time to make our move, you will know."

"Mr. Emir?" Candace asked. "Do you have something I can cover up with?"

Nodding, he walked down a hallway. Emir returned with a plush white bath sheet which he handed to Candace as he closed his eyes. She quickly wrapped herself in the warmth of the fabric.

"Thank you, Mr. Emir."

Again, he nodded his response and then slowly opened his eyes. "I am sorry for what I have to do with you now. I have to do as they say or they will be suspicious. I will check on you as much as I am allowed."

Emir walked around where Candace stood and entered a small yellow kitchen and retrieved a drinking glass from the light oak cabinet. He turned to the stainless-steel sink and filled it with water. "Here, please drink," Emir said as he handed the glass to her. She guzzled it, not realizing how thirsty she was and handed it back. He promptly refilled it a second time.

"Thank you, Sir," Candace said, quietly as she handed the glass back to Emir. "For being so kind. I'm so afraid. I just want to go home."

"I am so sorry for the way you are being treated," he replied, pity laced his words. "I have to put you in the takhzin now. I will return later with bread and water as I am able."

As he guided her to the rear of the house, passing a small dining table before opening the doors that led to the courtyard, Emir opened the takhzin's door.

"You must go in now. Please remain quiet and do not draw attention to this area," Emir warned. "I am not the only man who will guard this house, but I am the only man from Durabia. "You do not want them to be more aware of your presence," he closed the doors and left Candace wrapped only in the towel he had given her.

# Chapter 7

Jet lag hit Rory harder on this trip from Durabia than any of the others. His first stay was for a month; this time he spent six months. The time difference, combined with the long trip back to Birmingham, made for the most restful sleep Rory had experienced in a while once he stretched out in his own bed.

Rolling over to retrieve his phone from the charger, he read a missed text from his mother.

*Welcome home, son. I'm sorry I won't be there for brunch. Tarah and I are at Marcus' sister's house helping prepare for the celebration of life for their aunt. Have a great day. I can't wait to see your face.*

Putting the phone back on the nightstand, a little disappointed that he wouldn't get to see his mother this morning, Rory slid out from under the comforter and drifted to the balcony that overlooked Shades Creek Park and the campus of Samford University. Beautiful hills and valleys with lush greens, walking paths, and historical buildings surrounded the estate. The sun was peeking through the trees and the air was crisp and clean.

He loved this particular property because it was quiet and peaceful and allowed him to escape reality when he needed. Sometimes being immersed in the worst aspects of the world tore at his heart. No one understood why he put his life at risk to help total strangers. Khalil had done so for his mother. This afforded him a life that wouldn't be possible if they were living under the tyrannical authority of Anwar Futtaim. He would never have been able to own this home or any others if it wasn't for the opportunities Khalil Germaine had given him when he was growing up. He never understood what Khalil saw in him and would forever be in his debt for placing Rory and Malakai in Macro International in Chicago to study in their formative years.

Rory graduated from The University of Birmingham with a degree in finance. He worked to revitalize failing communities in the Birmingham area near Messer Airport Highway, inspired by the work of his close friend, Kaleb Valentine, King of South Shore.

Khalil had connected the two men early on because they had background situations that were similar in their need to stay under the radar. So much so, that Kaleb didn't even inform Rory when trouble in Chicago mounted and an old enemy resurfaced hellbent on putting Kaleb in the grave. Their first heated argument started because Kaleb didn't loop him in, instead turning solely to the new men that Khalil had pulled together. Rory could understand that those men were an immediate fix, but he should have trusted Rory enough to allow him to be there for him as well.

However, his efforts to breathe new life into a stagnant Birmingham had met with success. There were now thriving areas of the city that young families would be proud to call home. The improvements he made attracted small businesses through the Innovation Center, which was the hub of his community. In addition to the environmental enhancements, The Kings provided loans to area entrepreneurs through their foundations and organizations. With all of the loans paid in full, Rory was able to invest in other areas of Birmingham, setting him up for lifelong financial stability and ensuring that his family and close friends from college living on the estate were well taken care of.

When Khalil brought his family back to Alabama, it was hard on all of them. Rory's grandparents held resentment for his mother marrying his father. The story his mother told him still haunted him to this day.

*"Sweet boy," she whispered, stroking a hand through Rory's hair. "I*

*have to tell you how I was brought here in hopes you understand why we need to leave so suddenly and in such a secret way. So that you know the full story if something happens to me or we get separated," his mother said, her glassy, blue-eyed gaze wandering over his shoulder, checking the entrance. "My parents are what Christians call Southern Baptists. They wanted me to marry a rich white doctor, preferably the son of one of their country club friends. I met your father at my first and only job as a hostess at Rossman Bridge Golf Resort and Spa. Your father went by 'Jay' then. He was such a handsome man. Tan skin and thick dark hair. You look a lot like him now, even at twelve. You, too, will have girls chasing you when we're back in America, I'm sure."*

*Young Rory shuddered at the thought. Girls were the last thing on his mind. His mother's constant pain and fear took front and center of his thoughts. She believed she could hide the bruises, or even the fact that she couldn't walk faster than a snail's pace sometimes. He noticed everything and knew why. He had prayed for God to send help.*

*"Your father," she continued, bringing her gaze back to Rory whose eyes mirrored the ocean blue of her own. "He could have easily been a model. He was a smooth talker, but not a flirt. He treated me like a queen, even though I wasn't like the other girls who constantly sought his affections. They were extraordinarily beautiful and far more engaging".*

*Rory didn't understand those words because he thought his mother was elegant and beautiful.*

*"It was love at first sight. When I brought Jabir home to meet my parents for the first time, they were hospitable in the typical Southern way, carrying on a conversation with ease and tossing in the occasional 'Bless your heart'. But when he left, they warned that if I didn't stop seeing that 'Mexican' they would kick me out, and I would lose my inheritance. He wasn't Mexican of course, he was Emirati, just like you, but they only saw his darker skin.*

*Later, when I turned twenty-one, I broke the news that I was marrying Jabir and moving to Chicago to pursue my interior design program while your father ran his export businesses. They reluctantly attended the ceremony. My father told my mother that I was no longer his daughter as they left the wedding hall. He said it where I could hear him."*

*Tears streamed down her face, the first time Rory had seen his mother cry since his sister was born.*

*"Jabir took me to Durabia for our honeymoon and it was like a fairytale. When we were on our way to the airport for the trip back to Alabama to prepare for the big move to Chicago, Jabir had the transport detour into Nadaum. He said he had to meet with the man who had bought the majority stake in his company. That's when it hit me that he planned this deliberately, knowing I never would visit such a place, let alone want to live there. When we crossed that border and I screamed to the guard that I was being kidnapped, all Jabir had to show was that I was his wife and no one intervened. We arrived at this place, and he told me we were never leaving."*

*She held Rory to her bosom. "I've been held here, living under the Sharia Law. I was forced to abandon my Christian faith and become Muslim. I was forced to memorize the Koran or be beaten. I've been treated as though I'm a slave rather than a wife. I know you don't know this because you've never seen what marriage in the Western world looks like, but it's not supposed to be like this. A man should cherish and love his wife and treat her as though she is his queen, just like your father did when we first met." She closed her eyes and released a deep sigh before continuing.*

*"After several months of living in this hell, and you being my only joy, your father's employer Anwar Futtaim sent Jabir on many business trips. That is when Anwar started hurting me. The yelling and fighting at Malakai's seventh birthday party was when your father discovered that your brother was the fruit of Anwar's abuse." Tears streamed down her face as she shared her darkest secrets with Rory.*

*"Several years after that date, I was beaten every day your father was home, and taken advantage of by Anwar when he was gone. When I became pregnant with your sister, I feared for all of our lives as your father felt as if he had been betrayed again. Jabir was powerless against Anwar, and unable to take his frustrations out on the wealthy man who*

*violated me. So, he turned all of it on me, convinced I would bear another child of the man he hated. I don't know how we survived."*

*She explained that Anwar's sister Nadara was the only kind adult in her life. "When she saw how bad things had become, and that I would surely meet my end, she told me I needed to get my family out of Nadaum or I wouldn't live to see your sister's next birthday, let alone my sons grow into men. She handed me a card with a name: Khalil Germaine."*

Rory's phone rang, snapping him out of his reverie, and he returned to his bedroom.

"Luis, what's up?" Rory said when he answered, sliding on the clean pair of joggers that his staff had laid out on an antique chest of drawers.

"Hermano," Luis greeted as if they were still friends. "Welcome back. How was Durabia?"

"Excellent." Rory smiled at the thought of the women who were now safe and situated in a shelter run by a sister to the current reigning Sheikh Kamran and his wife, along with some of the Knights who now resided in Durabia.

The night that his mother decided to run to Durabia to escape his father was one of the scariest of his life. Rory had just turned twelve, Malakai was nine, and Tarah was just a toddler of eighteen months. His mother had told him what would happen, but did not explain it to Malakai, who would not keep secrets from Futtaim as he always lavished him with presents and attention. His past helped him understand the fear and distrust that the women he now helped experienced all the way up to the moment they realized they were actually safe.

"Durabia is a lot of work," Rory explained. "My center is open, and we already have thirty residents."

"That's great, Rory. Really awesome," Luis stated with a hint of sarcasm. "You're *such* an honorable man."

A chill snaked up Rory's spine. Not that he wasn't deserving of the compliment, but it almost sounded as if Luis was mocking him.

"So, what can I do for you *Prosecutor Fry?*" Rory questioned, emphasizing his title as a jab at his old friend who was on the verge of becoming a foe again. In college, Luis' competitive nature surfaced in everything from grades to social settings. Rory couldn't help that he took his studies more seriously than Luis, and his accolades and final results always aimed him toward success. Luis was too busy being up under the skirts that lifted for him and being in trouble for the ones that didn't. After the last allegations of sexual assault came to light, Rory refused to lie and say that Luis was in the dorm at the time. Rory distanced himself from Luis and he didn't take it well. No way in hell would Rory consider a man who tried to force himself on a woman a friend. However, he did plan to be cordial for etiquette's sake.

"Man, I just wanted to make sure you received my invite to the Gala. I want to see you. I'm doing big things, just like you."

"I'll be there. Tomorrow night, right? Fundraiser for The Wellbound House?"

"Yes sir, that's the one. It'll be great to see you. Be there at seven."

"Got it." Rory put his phone down to retrieve a shirt. He didn't even have it all the way over his head when the phone rang again. "Didn't take you long, did it?"

"Welcome home," Daron Kincaid said. "Glad to know you made it back safely."

Daron, King of Morgan Park, happened to be The Castle's tech guru and digital genius. He invented tracking devices that helped find victims of human trafficking. Rory first met Daron when he came back to Marco International School in Chicago to give a motivational speech to a group of boys after he graduated from the University of Birmingham. Rory didn't have a great role model in his father, so he was indebted to Khalil for everything that he'd done since rescuing his family. That's when he was introduced to Daron and Kaleb Valentine, who both took Rory under their wings, helping him build the foundation for his business ventures in Birmingham.

*All of the Kings are powerful, strong men who do good across the world with their fortune and ventures. I'm happy to be in such good company.*

"Are you ready for your next assignment?"

Rory yawned and stretched before releasing a sigh. He wasn't ready to jump back in yet. He wanted to catch up with his family, but knew he didn't have a choice. What he gleaned from the files Daron sent before Rory boarded the plane, is that was going down would happen in the next week or two. Rory would have only a short amount of time to figure things out. "What's going on," he asked, making his way to the dressing area of his bathroom. "Where do you need me?"

Daron chuckled. "I know you were hoping to have a couple of days off, but something's come up. Tomorrow night there's a gala fundraiser for The Wellbound House at a place called Rossman Bridge."

Rory processed Daron's statement for a few seconds, trying to figure out how all of this fell into place so quickly. "I just got off the phone with Luis Fry confirming my attendance."

"Excellent. Something is going on down there, and we're trying to get to the bottom of it before we lose a way to connect to key players. We think the DA, a prosecutor named—" Daron paused for a moment, and the sound of papers shifting could be heard on the other end. "Oh, Luis Fry, the guy you just mentioned. Wellbound is also involved somehow. Women are missing from the state prisons and transitional homes sponsored by The Journey Beyond. Find Meghan Turner, I'll text you her picture and all the information we could find on such short notice. Tell her Daron from the Castle sent you. I'll be in Birmingham shortly. We'll talk more then."

Rory wasn't sure what to make of all this. Luis could be shady, but he didn't think he would be mixed up in anything nefarious. He remembered the party that kept Malakai out all night and wondered if all of these events were associated. "You got it, Daron. See you soon."

Disconnecting the call, he glanced at the picture of Meghan Turner that came through. He scrolled through the dossier, then searched online for more information on her and the organization. But his attention kept returning to her photo. Her long, wavy auburn hair and striking blue eyes caught Rory's attention right away. He'd never seen eyes the color of the most perfect blue sky. Her serious smile gave her an angelic glow. The white, button-down shirtdress hugged her voluptuous figure beautifully. A sparkling circle on a silver chain glistened just above the top of the unfastened button as though her halo had been misplaced. She appeared to be gazing into his very soul.

Rory's heart beat faster as he stared at the screen, as if he and the woman in the picture were connected on some level. Mixing business with pleasure never ended well. Besides, he didn't have time for love on top of learning his role in The Castle and how he fit in with the Kings.

Blasting *Free Me* by the Foo Fighters on his Bose system, Rory strutted down the hall to his home gym and pushed himself to the limit in an effort to erase the distraction now burned into his mind—Meghan Turner.

# Chapter 8

Within the hour, Jefferson County Sheriff, Mack Johnson, and State Prosecutor, Luis Fry, were in Meghan's office sitting at the small conference table she'd acquired after the shutdown of a school on the city's North side.

Meghan and Sally were on one side, and Johnson and Fry were on the other, as though each team were presenting a united front. Maria wasn't present for the meeting. She'd mentioned a court appointment, but nothing on her office calendar bore that out. She wasn't responding to Sally's calls or Meghan's texts.

"Thank you for coming on short notice Sheriff Johnson, and Luis," Meghan said, trying to remain calm even though her concern for Candace was ever-present on her mind.

District Attorney Willingham and Sheriff Johnson had accused her of being too emotional when she'd interned at the D.A.'s office. Once after a particularly tough debate in the middle of a court case, he tossed that accusation out there to embarrass her in front of a room filled with their colleagues and she shot back, "So when you were pissed off at your deputy and turned over his desk, was that passion or emotion? When you 'accidentally' put a warning shot at your wife because she had asked for a divorce, was that passion or emotion? I just want to be clear about things so I can act accordingly." The judge laughed so hard he slid from the bench and had to call for a recess. Willingham had it out for Meghan ever since and his cronies had picked up that baton. She was grateful Willingham wasn't with the other two gentlemen today. He certainly would have made things more complicated.

"We have a serious problem, that needs to be addressed," Meghan said, flickering a gaze to Sally so she could take the lead.

"We've noticed something interesting with our cases," Sally explained as she interlaced her stubby fingers and placed her hands on top of the folders on the table. "Since we started seeing a trend in these cases, I created files on all of the women who seem to fit the profile of who are missing and did background research on each one." She paused a minute, as though giving the men an opportunity to either speak or make an initial comment. Meghan certainly needed a moment because she was aware of the missing women and the initial documents, but knew nothing of the additional efforts that Sally had taken to keep track of things.

"Ages nineteen to twenty-nine, Black women with light complexions or Hispanic women with slightly darker ones. Single with no family to advocate for them, slender builds, and remarkably beautiful." She tossed a folder in front of the Sheriff and Luis, who took their time opening to the first page.

"I compiled files for each of the women with documents and information found online—their pictures and anything else I could uncover," Sally explained with a pointed look at the men whose expressions remained stoic. "I'm trying to uncover more, but what we know now is at least nine of these women are now missing."

"Candace Simmons is one of those women," Meghan added, holding back tears. Pride wouldn't allow her to let Luis or Sheriff Johnson see her vulnerable, as their poker buddies would certainly get wind of it. She waited until they turned to the next page and another woman's smiling face beamed up at them. "I went to make my scheduled visit, and she was gone. When I inquired further, it was as if she'd never been there."

Luis was well aware of who Candace was. He'd prosecuted her case as though she was a hardened criminal, and he was behind the lengthy sentence she'd been given. Meghan couldn't help but think that he treated Candace differently because of her relationship with Meghan. The women first met as children in the schoolyard in Bessemer, but Candace's life had taken a decidedly different turn when she hooked up with a man who ran with the "B-ham Gladiators" street gang. Luis used the young woman as a pawn to strike back at Meghan.

Refusing to continue sleeping with a man who was building a power base county and statewide did have its disadvantages. But she never wanted anyone to think she'd slept her way to the top. Well, in his case, the bottom because only lately he was spiraling upward. Back then, he was an unknown.

"I don't have a file on Candace because she didn't fit the profile." Sally sucked in a deep breath, releasing a gust of air. "Candace and the other women were somehow wiped from the system, but everyone in this room knows they exist because they ended up on the wrong end of your radar and political aspirations," she said, holding up a flash drive. "Maybe you can take this to someone up the chain and show them this issue bears looking into. These are copies of official documents."

Meghan resisted commenting because at the moment, she was wondering how long Sally had been tracking everything. Evidently, Meghan needed to be more aware of what was happening in the office instead of out trying to raise funds. She had to be at the forefront of the fundraising that kept the doors open. But they wouldn't remain that way for long if women distanced themselves from JB because it was entrenched in political muck and shrouded in shadowy and wicked purposes.

"We want the originals," Luis demanded, finally finding his voice.

"Why?"

"To make sure they weren't altered," he shot back, glaring at her as though she should have known his reasoning "In this day and age, anything is possible."

"Well, start with what you have," she countered, holding up a hand to stave off Sally's response. "When it becomes necessary to produce them because you've found something viable, then we'll turn them over."

"What? You don't trust us?" the sheriff asked, his head tilted as his beady green eyes narrowed to slits.

"Trust has nothing to do with it," Meghan said in the coldest voice she could manage. "But if it becomes necessary to hand it over to the FBI, I don't want to have to explain to them why they aren't in my possession."

"The FBI?" Luis said, smirking. "We don't need to involve them."

"You might be right," Meghan said, reaching over to turn the page since he seemed uninterested in doing so. She tapped the edge of the document bringing his focus to yet another woman. "We'll give you a first crack at the case. We wouldn't want to be accused of not following protocol."

"We'll have to take this back to the courthouse and sort through it," the sheriff said, glaring at Sally while putting a hand on Luis' shoulder to halt any further protest. "Something isn't right. Your records must be wrong."

"Everything is here for you on this USB drive," Sally said, handing them a purple drive with the JB logo on it.

Sally never trusted the law after what she'd been through.

Meghan wasn't surprised.

# Chapter 9

Long after her normal lunch hour, Maria Sanchez tipped in the back door of the office. She froze upon hearing Meghan and Sally speaking with two men whose voices sounded familiar. She inched closer to the door and placed her back against the wall so she wouldn't be seen. Her heart slammed against her chest when she realized what they were discussing.

She knew exactly what was happening with the missing women. Luis Fry had cornered her in court last month after a particularly tough case where one of her clients was denied bail. The court also dissolved her parental rights with breakneck speed, allowing the family fostering her three young kids to adopt them. The move pretty much guaranteed she would never see them again.

Erika Coleman had left her three children at home alone under the watch of her oldest daughter so she wouldn't have to miss her shift at the auto parts plant, the only source of income to feed her family. Her oldest, Chloe, was nine. No Alabama law existed that said the minimum age children could be without parental supervision. Erika didn't do it often, but on that fateful night she had no choice when the babysitter cancelled last minute.

Unfortunately, two-year-old Michael fell down the stairs of their two-story home in Pell City and broke his wrist. Chloe couldn't reach Erika because cell phones weren't allowed on her job. When she arrived at the house, her kids were gone, and the police were waiting. The speed with which they processed her case showed the efficiency of a system set up to prevent Black women from ever breaking the cycle. After the judge and the prosecution effectively crushed Erika's hopes, Maria left the courtroom and made her way toward the restroom to pull herself together. But Luis Fry, attorney for the prosecution, tapped her shoulder before she could slide through the door.

*"What do you want?" Maria asked with a hint of disdain in her voice. He had this used car salesman vibe about him that had always made her uneasy, despite the designer suits and eloquent way of speaking.*

*"Is that any way to talk to a prosecutor, someone you have to negotiate with, Ms. Sanchez?"*

*Maria rolled her eyes and turned to leave the courthouse. Her kidneys could wait until she made it back to JB.*

*"I need to speak to you," he insisted, falling in step with her hurried pace.*

*Maria slowly turned around, leveling a hard gaze on him. "What. Do. You. Want?"*

*Luis chuckled and pointed to a small boardroom near the criminal courtroom they'd just exited. He wasn't a tall man, but he had a strong, intimidating presence. Like Maria, he was of blended parentage—White and Puerto Rican. His dark hair with the tiniest bit of salt complemented a complexion so smooth it was obvious he was hitting the spa as well as the gym. He was maturing early, though he wasn't quite forty, and wore it well. The issue, in her eyes, was that he had enough connections to make himself someone to be feared.*

*Luis followed Maria into the dark room, waving a hand under the sensor to activate the lights.*

*Maria hesitated as she settled into the chair at the head of the conference table and glared at Luis who was perched on the opposite end wearing what she thought had to be a custom-made dark gray suit, because nothing off the rack would fit his short, but athletic build so perfectly.*

*She forced herself to look away because she was not ever going to think of this man with any feelings other than hate. What he did to her people - his own people, Hispanics and Blacks in Birmingham – was a disgrace. He could use the power he wielded in his position as a minority politician to help his community, but that wouldn't line his pockets and buy designer clothes.*

*"Maria, you are going to help me," Luis said with a sheepish grin.*

*Didn't ask, didn't make a request. Simply told her that she was going to do something. Her hackles automatically went up.*

*"I'm working with a very important man in Nadaum," Luis said. "He's interested in obtaining some of Alabama's finest women who have been tragically locked up. You know, give them a hand up in life, get them out of prison in exchange for some lucrative work. However, the United States has strict guidelines that are making it difficult for us to accomplish this humanitarian effort."*

*Maria tried to hide her concern for what she believed he was alluding to without coming out and saying it straight and true. "What do I have to do with any of this? I'm not on anyone's radar, and I don't have nearly the power that you do."*

*Luis moved until he was directly behind Maria. He placed his hands on her shoulders and began rubbing them as if he had suddenly become a long-lost lover.*

*She shrugged him off. "No me toques," she growled in Spanish, telling him not to touch her.*

*He laughed and leaned over so his cheek was next to hers as he spoke in a whisper, "Oh, but you are going to help me, mi amor. The only answer is yes, if you want tu madre y hermana to see this side of Tutwiler."*

*Maria's heart plummeted in response to his thinly-veiled threat to her mother and sister who were serving time for killing her father.*

*"So this is how it will work."*

*Luis proceeded to explain Maria's new unwanted support role, then ended with, "For tu familia to stay safe while they're serving hard time, you will tell no one. I promise, they will feel every ounce of any betrayal. And—," he stroked a hand across her face causing her to flinch, "you will be tested. I suggest you stick to the plan. I'll be in touch."*

*Luis slid a burner phone across the table and walked out of the conference room, leaving Maria behind with more problems that she had when she walked into court.*

"Maria is that you?" Meghan asked from JB's conference room door "Please come in here. We've been trying to reach you. It's urgent."

Maria trudged through the door separating the front from the rear of the office. Her heart sank to the bottom of her stomach when she saw the sheriff and none other than Luis Fry himself giving her that signature smug look that made her stomach churn.

"Before the sheriff and Mr. Fry leave, we need to tell you what's going on, in case you have information to share," Sally explained, giving Maria a side eye. "There are women associated with The Journey Beyond who are missing from the Tutwiler Prison and some of the group homes. One of them is Candace Simmons."

Maria wanted to bolt for the door and run straight out of the building. Candace must have been the test that Fry had mentioned. Now she had to choose between endangering her family, who had killed her father in order to save her life, or betraying the one person who had given her a chance to free them.

Luis knew exactly what Candace meant to Meghan. Maria didn't know what he had against her, but it was clear something was driving his actions because this reeked of revenge. It broke her heart to see what Meghan was going through, knowing she had a hand in it somehow. Still, she had to protect her sister and mother from whatever Luis was capable of doing to them.

Betraying him could end their lives. And hers.

# Chapter 10

Meghan was exhausted after a long day at court and the meeting in the office that didn't produce the results needed to make her confident that Candace and those other women would be found. Something felt off with Maria, but she couldn't pinpoint exactly what.

Maria had been distracted ever since the meeting with the Sheriff and DA. She came out of the back room of the office as Sally was handing Meghan the files on the missing girls. Maria flinched, and her face pulled into a withdrawn, almost hollow look. She walked to her desk with her head down, avoiding eye contact with everyone. Her actions were those of a guilty person. But guilty of what?

"Maria, are you doing okay?" Sally asked during their afternoon meeting. "You seem distracted."

"I'm fine." Maria snapped, squaring her shoulders in a defensive posture.

"How many cases do you have scheduled next week, Maria?" Meghan asked.

"Six," she replied, still unwilling to make eye contact. Instead, her gaze was on the electronic tablet in her hands.

"Do you need anything from us?" Sally asked, peering at her with the same suspicion that Meghan felt. "Any guidance? Mentoring?"

"No," Maria said with a haughty lift of her chin.

For the rest of the conversation, Maria was short and curt in discussing her cases. They were no more aware of her status than when she first walked in.

As soon as their meeting concluded, Maria shoved the folders into her bag, scrambled out of her seat, and was out the door without saying anything more.

"Well that was strange," Sally said, her focus still on the space that Maria had vacated. "She's been acting like this since dumb and dumber were here."

Meghan was three steps ahead of that thought and was on to why. "I wonder if she's worried about her sister. I'll ask her. Do me a favor and text her about the gala since she left before we could tell her. She should be there."

Sally nodded, and Meghan gathered her things.

"And text me the plans too," she added. "See you tomorrow."

The Journey Beyond had purchased several tickets for the annual fundraiser for the Wellbound, a human trafficking rescue in Birmingham. She hadn't made plans to attend because she would rather eat dirt than spend time with fake politicians and even more fake society people who didn't give a rat's ass about Wellbound, JB, or the women they serviced. They simply wanted an excuse to show off their over-the-top jewelry and designer garments because the cameras would be rolling.

With everything going on with the missing women, Lisa Montoya, Sally's partner, had arranged for an outside organization to help investigate.

"We received an email from the DA not even an hour after those two clowns left, stating that there was no record of any of the missing women and threatening legal action for costing taxpayers money if we continue in this line of investigation. I told Lisa what was going on," Sally explained in an effort to accentuate why Meghan had to get over her misgivings and attend the Gala.

"She's connected to some pretty powerful people. You know, Lisa moved from Chicago to Alabama about a year ago. When she was in Chicago, she was living in a shelter after escaping an abusive relationship," Sally further explained. "The shelter was amazing, like living in a luxury apartment complex. Lisa told me they took care of everything, including health and mental health care. I told her everything at dinner last night. That was before I knew you were bringing Thing One and Thing Two. She was so upset, she reached out to someone named Mariano DeLuca who operated the shelter. He called her right back and Lisa put the phone on speaker. I told him about Candace and the other missing women."

Meghan leaned the side of her head against her hand, her elbow resting on the metal desk as she stared at Sally in wide-eyed disbelief. "Sally, you can't just go sharing this information with strangers," she said, alarmed that her partner had brought in a faction that she hadn't sanctioned. "We already don't know enough about what's going on. Why does a guy in Chicago care about anything that's going on in Alabama, anyway?"

Sally shook her head, her guarded expression spoke of her frustration. "They aren't *really* strangers if they're coming to help. Bless your heart and take a breath will ya? Don't you trust me by now? Anyway, this DeLuca said he's got an associate in Alabama and would put him on it right away." Sally held out her phone so Meghan could see the screen. "He messaged me before our meeting this afternoon and said his name is Rory Tannous and he'll find you. You will know it's him because he'll say The Castle sent him."

Meghan plucked the phone from Sally's hand and read the rest of the message.

*Tell Meghan to trust him and the three of you should find a place to talk so you can fill him in. He'll take it from there.*

Meghan let out a long, slow breath realizing that her suspicions might not be so far off. Luis Fry had recently been appointed to the board of The Wellbound House. She couldn't fathom why they would want representation from the man responsible for putting so many of their clients in jail. Same reason she bolted at the idea that the director of the government agency providing grants to JB insisted he have some involvement in her organization in an "oversight" capacity. She found it disturbing that Luis took such pleasure in locking up young women of color. Meghan couldn't make sense of it, especially considering he was also of Hispanic lineage.

Meghan pulled up in front of the quaint apartment building in Homewood just outside of Birmingham. The area was safer than the neighborhoods in the city she could afford to live in as a single woman. The bonus was that it was also not too far from her office. She didn't have to get on a highway to make it into work, which was great, because every interchange was a nightmare during commuting hours.

She parked her Highlander on the street in front of the building and walked up the sidewalk leading to her garden studio apartment. Her steps slowed when she noticed a document had been taped to the painted green door.

Meghan scanned the block to see if anyone was in the area before snatching it down. Unlocking the door, she walked in and dropped her bag on the couch before opening the note.

*Leave it alone.*

That was all it said. No signature, no letterhead. No indication of who sent it.

"What the hell?" Meghan whispered as she tossed the note on the table. Leave what alone? Her heart raced like a train about to jump the tracks. She put her head in her hands and steadied her breathing, then a knock at her door grabbed her attention.

Meghan searched the small space for anything she could use to protect herself. She made a mental note to buy a steel bat that next time she went out. She then realized she hadn't locked her door after entering, rushed to the couch and grabbed a broom leaning against the arm. Inching to the door, she peered through the peep hole then let out a sigh of relief when she recognized Sue Ellyn, her nosy and possibly bipolar elderly landlord. *Thank God.*

She put the broom in a corner and opened the door. "Hi Sue Ellyn," Meghan greeted with a nervous smile. "How are you today, ma'am?"

A warm smile spread across Sue Ellyn's wrinkled face as she stood across the threshold in a housedress that matched the bright yellow, green, and blue hues of the building. Her silver curls were tight to her head, and she wore her signature bright red lipstick. She was a spry, eighty-year-old woman, and a bit eccentric.

*She will go to her grave with those red lips.*

"Hello sweet girl," Sue Ellyn replied, glancing past Meghan into her apartment. "I saw you walking in. You look so tired. Are you doing okay?"

Meghan sighed and angled so the woman could come in, but wondered if she had seen the person who had plastered that warning on the door. "It's been a very long week, but I'm fine. I'm going to have a little whiskey and relax for the rest of the evening. For a little while, I'd like to think about something other than work. How are you?"

Sue Ellyn clasped her hands together in front of her and pursed her lips. "I'm doing well Meghan, but I need to speak to you about a visitor you had today."

Meghan's heart rate took another uptick. "A visitor? I wasn't expecting any visitors today. Did you speak to them?"

Sue Ellyn shook her head as she leaned against the edge of the doorframe. They still stood in the entrance with the door wide open since Sue Ellyn hadn't accepted the offer to enter the apartment. "They banged on your door so loud I swear every dog in the building was barking. I walked out to see what the commotion was about, and those hoodlums gave me the middle finger. They drove a rusty old red truck with a big confederate flag flying." She fanned a weathered hand in front of her nose. "And stunk like cigarettes and bad weed." She leaned forward to whisper. "Trust me, I know what the good stuff smells like. Have some in the house."

*Well that explains it.*

They looked like them there Bradland Boys, if you know what I mean."

Bradland was an Alabama town made up of mostly run-down trailer parks where stereotypical rednecks lived. The only jobs left in Bradland were at the cement plant, and it was going out of business. The town was known for three things—racists, inbreeding, and meth labs. Chief Richards ran the "sundown" town along with one other police officer. Bradland was nowhere a person of color should ever travel unless that person had a death wish. Evidently, she had made it on their radar and warranted a special delivery.

*Leave it alone.*

Meghan knew the group of men Sue Ellyn was talking about, as some of their wives walked through the doors of JB for help from time to time. Only difference, those women went back every single time.

Putting the old woman at ease, Meghan said, "I don't know anyone like that, ma'am. I'm so sorry they caused a disturbance here." She took the weathered hands in her own and gave a gentle squeeze. "Please let me know if you see them again. Better yet, if you do, call the cops." She sighed, mulling over her next steps. "I'll call and speak to the Homewood Chief tomorrow morning and ask for extra patrols around here just to be safe. Thanks for letting me know."

Sue Ellyn's tense posture relaxed a little. "I was hoping they weren't of your relation. Make sure to lock your door tonight, Miss Meghan. I'm going to go now. Goodnight."

Meghan watched Sue Ellyn until she made it to her home, then closed and latched her door.

She hoped whoever left the note was at the wrong apartment. Because if it was a message that she was supposed to understand, they had failed. Miserably. What should she leave alone? Maybe one of her clients was related to them.

Hoping to set her own mind at ease, Meghan sent a quick text to Chief Brian Carrolton, a friend and the chief of Homewood PD, to call her when he had a minute. They had a decent relationship since he was good friends with Mama Ann and Mama Tee. She'd give him the rundown of what went down and let him decide if they should send extra patrols.

Meghan put her phone on silent as she locked the door, closed all the blinds, and hit the button on her key fob one more time to make sure her car doors were locked.

# Chapter 11

Walking into his estate after an afternoon of running errands for his mother and sister Tarah, Rory was grateful to see his friends Marcus and James playing Uno Flip with James' oldest son Jeffrey, Tarah, and his mother Chrissy at the table in Rory's large dining room. Malakai was missing in action, something Rory discovered had become a regular occurrence.

"Rory," Marcus and James exclaimed in unison jumping up to help him with the grocery bags from Publix Market. "No guys, I've got it. Sit and continue your game, it looks like Tarah is kicking your butts."

Rory laughed, and his mother embraced him. His sister looked up at him with her big beautiful smile.

At twenty-three, Tarah's brain operated on the level of a twelve-year-old. She was diagnosed with Autism at the age of three, a little over a year after they escaped Nadaum. Chrissy was devastated and unsure how she would care for a special needs child as a single mother. Rory believed that Allah blessed their family with Tarah to help them slow down and appreciate the important things in life. Tarah was different, but she was all love.

"Big brother," Tarah squealed, before jumping up and hugging Rory after he conceded to Marcus and James' insistence on relieving him of the grocery haul. She was not affectionate as a rule, but sometimes she surprised everyone. Especially when it came to her interactions with Rory.

"I've missed you. Sit now, play Uno with us so I can beat you too." Tarah pulled on Rory's arm in an attempt to guide him into a chair beside her.

"But don't look at my cards," she warned before snatching her hand and hiding it from Rory's view.

"Okay, if you—"

Rory's phone vibrated. He pulled it from his pocket and glanced at the screen. Mariano DeLuca "Reno" flashed as it continued to buzz.

"Tarah, I'm so sorry, I have to take this."

Tarah gave her brother her saddest puppy dog eyes as he excused himself and walked through the dining area into the kitchen where Marcus and James were putting the groceries away.

"King Reno," Rory answered. "Long time no talk. How can I help you?"

"It's good to hear your voice," Reno replied. "I received a call from a woman who works with Meghan Turner. Sally Decker. Do you know her or Lisa Montoya?"

"The names don't sound familiar."

"Well, It seems Meghan's been targeted by a group of men from a place called Bradland. Have you heard of that place?"

"Yes. There are some problematic people in that area," Rory answered, thinking about the White Supremacist groups that have called Bradland home for the last decade or so. "Bradland is home to several of them."

All it took was the mention of Bradland for Marcus and James to excuse themselves and return to the game. Rory moved beyond the kitchen, making his way to the door next to his office that led outside to the gardens.

One particular militia group of both older men and younger recruits, took issue with Rory when he started transforming communities in

Birmingham. They didn't like white folks lending a hand to people of color. They called him an abomination and vandalized many of the properties with graffiti and stole copper fittings and appliances, costing Rory and his team both time and money on the progress of the project in North Birmingham.

"I read about Meghan's organization when Daron sent me her info. She helps incarcerated women of color, right?" Rory asked, peering out of the window before stepping outside to let the warmth of the sun hit him full-on.

"That's right. And it's those same women who are missing," Reno confirmed.

Rory shook his head. "Things are worse than I imagined then. If the Bradland Boys are targeting Meghan, she's in more trouble than we thought." He dropped onto one of the comfy chairs and propped his feet up on the cushioned ottoman. "Which Kings will be at the Gala?"

Before finishing their conversation, Rory and Reno discussed the logistics of the Gala and planned a preliminary strategy based on what little they knew.

"Go spend the evening with your family," Reno suggested. "Tomorrow we'll get to work."

Rory disconnected the call, tucking all of the information into his memory bank.

"Tarah, that is not how you play this game, young lady, and you know it." Rory returned to the dining area where the game continued with James schooling Tarah on Uno manners. She wasn't having it because she wanted to win by any means she felt necessary.

"I'm making dinner tonight," he said, realizing that James and Marcus had Tarah well in hand. They were always so patient. "My favorite chicken curry recipe from Durabia. Who wants to help?" Chrissy jumped up, thrilled at the opportunity to spend some time in the kitchen with her son.

Rory kissed her temple, then handed over the folded piece of paper he'd retrieved from his pocket that contained the recipe for their meal.

"I'm so glad to have you home, son," Chrissy exclaimed her eyes alight with joy, before she reached into the cupboards and gathered the ingredients.

Rory flashed a smile, stopping his mother's leisurely steps to wrap her in his arms. "I'm glad to be back." Releasing her, he bent down to grab the pots and pans from a cabinet and set them on the stove. "Where's Malakai? He's been scarce since I've been back."

"I don't know," Chrissy responded with a bit of sadness in her voice. "He's here and then he's not a lot of the time. He doesn't even tell me when he leaves."

They spent the next hour cooking, catching up on how her work at the literacy center, and laughing while preparing what Rory hoped would be the first of many family meals while he was back home.

Only vaguely did he wonder about Malakai and his strange disappearances since he had arrived on American soil.

# Chapter 12

Malakai was preparing for a game of three on three basketball at Lifetime Fitness when a man he had never seen at the gym walked into the locker room. Given the man's girth, this wasn't his first choice for staying fit.

"Malakai," the man's thick accented bass voice bounced off the empty lockers as he spoke.

"Do I know you?" Malakai asked, narrowing his gaze on the man's unfamiliar features.

"Unfortunately no, thanks to Chrissy Tannous," the man said.

"How do you know my mother?" Malakai asked, taking a more careful look at this man who seemed to know him and his mother, but was a stranger. Wearing a Milano Gray Zegna suit over his stocky frame, he certainly wasn't dressed for a workout. His dark brown hair was sprinkled with salt showing that he was maturing. The neatly trimmed beard framed a round face with dark brown eyes that, upon closer inspection, strongly resembled his own.

"My name is Anwar Futtaim and I am your father."

"That isn't possible, sir, my father has been gone a very long time. He went off for a work assignment and was killed," Malakai responded, disgusted that anyone would make such a claim about his lineage.

"I am aware of Jabir's status. I was taking care of your mother while he was away on business for me. He … harmed your mother when he found out that I was your biological father/ That is why he met his demise before your mother stole you from your home. And from me."

Malakai couldn't believe what he was hearing. Who the hell did this man think he was? This had to be some sort of prank. The only one he confided in about his family was Luis, who was already late for today's game.

"Luis sent you, didn't he? This is one of his stupid jokes," Malakai growled, frustrated at the presence of this man.

"No, my son. Luis did not send me to prank you. I speak the truth."

Anwar Futtaim moved closer to Malakai, extending his hand to shake which Malakai rejected. Pulling out his phone, Malakai texted Luis.

*Where are you? You're late.*

A few moments after Malakai hit send, Luis bounced into the locker room.

"Ah, I see Futtaim beat me here," Luis said, with a smug look in Futtaim's direction. "Looks like you two have met. Did you share the good news?"

"You knew about this?" Malakai asked, as anger nearly caused him to say something more disrespectful.

"How do you think Anwar found you? We've been working together for years and it wasn't until you shared your family history over tequila to break in your new home last month that it dawned on me." He placed a hand on Malakai's shoulder. "You could be his son and very helpful to us. So, I pulled a few strings at state department, thanks to good connections, and what do you know, you are the long-lost son Anwar has been searching for."

Luis shared that information as though he was proud of himself for dismantling Malakai's entire world.

Malakai glanced over Anwar's shoulder to the mirror that stretched over part of the wall. Anwar angled to follow what had caught Malakai's attention. He smiled at their mutual reflections. Even if Malakai wanted to disregard this man, the proof was right there in front of him.

How many other lies had she told them? And why would she keep him from a man who was so obviously wealthy, when they had lived so modestly before Rory came into a knightship that changed their lives.

Why did Rory have all the luck? With women? With money? In having their mother's love? Why couldn't Malakai have been worthy of those things? He was smart, too. Well, despite the fact that Khalil Germaine had Malakai escorted out of Macro due to not trying to handle the curriculum. Why should he work so hard when Rory already had money enough to support them?

He couldn't let on to Anwar that he believed his claims. Malakai had to question what his life had been if she had taken him for some other reason than this man asserted.

"This is bullshit. I'm leaving." Malakai stormed out, unsure of what his next move would be. He had never had a strong relationship with his father—correction—the man he always believed to be his father before they left Nadaum under the cover of darkness. He had to speak to his mother.

# Chapter 13

Unzipping her skirt as she made her way to the restroom, Meghan started the water in the large garden tub, lit a lavender-scented candle, and poured a glass of Jameson from the minibar near the chaise lounge in the coastal themed space. She probably could afford a more expensive place, if she didn't sink most of her money into the organization. Mama Tee and Mama Ann had set that trust to release funds every five years until Meghan turned fifty. Probably a good thing since a lump sum would've already been in JB's account with no type of nest egg for Meghan later in life. Non-profit work was mentally, spiritually, and emotionally rewarding, but it was hell on the finances.

She needed to clear her mind of all the recent activities so she could devise a plan to find Candace and the other missing women. Not that she didn't trust that Sally had the best intentions, but she didn't know Mariano DeLuca or Rory Tannous personally and wasn't going to hang her hat on how effective these men would be. Especially since they were so far removed from the problems at hand. She was much more interested in figuring out if Maria Sanchez had anything to do with what was going on. She would take Sally's direction for now and attend the Gala and meet with this Rory person, but when everything was said and done, she would still depend on herself to see things through.

Meghan checked her phone once more before heading back to the bedroom. Chief Carrolton had called, and she'd missed it. As she dialed him back, Meghan released a calming breath.

"Meg, how are you, darlin'?" Chief Carrolton asked, his tone full of southern charm.

She smiled at the comforting sound of his voice. Ever since she had lost her father, Chief Carrolton was a constant male presence in her life. She considered him family along with Mama Ann and Mama Tee.

"Chief, things are a mess right now," Meghan explained, pulling down her Murphy bed and taking a seat on the edge. "I can't get into all of it, because I'm slap worn out and need to rest before this gala tomorrow. I need to share something that happened at my apartment today and get your opinion."

"Okay darling, go ahead," Chief Carrolton assured, and the rustling of pages being shuffled on the opposite end signaled he was still at the station. "I'm all ears."

Meghan told the chief about the Bradland Boys, then asked, "Should I be worried?"

"Darling, I'll see to it that my officers do some extra patrols.," the chief responded, his voice laced with concern. "Probably should have Jack sit in the cul-de-sac and watch that stop sign anyway. We make a killing on that spot every week. Please call me right away if anything else happens. And let's have coffee sometime so we can chat."

"Thank you Chief," Meghan said. "I'll be sure to stay in touch."

She placed her phone on the breakfast bar beside her bed and ran to the bathroom. The water was trickling over the tub's edge onto the green and blue retro tile floor. "Shit, shit, shit."

Meghan turned the water off then grabbed some towels and dropped them at her feet. She took a sip of whiskey and decided she'd already made a mess, so she was getting in anyway. She pulled the plug to lower the water level some.

She slipped out of her skirt and slid the purple top over her head. Standing in front of a white cheval mirror, she admired the curves of her body—wavy red tresses that framed her freckled collar bones. Speckles she once despised, but now loved every tiny mark. She pivoted so her angle in the mirror gave her a view of the rounded back side that swept into a small waist. Meghan admired that part of her body nearly as much as her past lovers did.

Stepping into the tub, the hot water swallowed her achy body. Listening to the water spill over the tub, Meghan believed the towels would do their job and she didn't have to worry about any damage that might happen to the floor.

She needed the water, the quiet, and the warm sensation of whiskey flowing through her veins in order to shut down for the evening. Meghan took a generous sip, allowing herself to feel the sting of the alcohol on her tongue before slowly swallowing the amber liquid, feeling the warmth spread throughout her body after it slid down her throat.

Meghan closed her eyes and inhaled the calming scent of lavender from the candle she lit before taking the call with the Chief. The tension ebbed from her shoulders all the way to her toes, and she drifted off, turning her mind off and succumbing to her exhaustion with one last question on her mind.

*Who was Rory Tannous?*

# *Chapter 14*

Chrissy was in the kitchen making Kunefe—Malakai's favorite, a Middle Eastern dessert that held layers of flaky phyllo dough, soaked in syrup. She had been surprised to receive the text asking for some one-on-one time. Even though they lived in the same home, she rarely saw her younger son.

She had noticed an increasing difference in him the more successful Rory became. She had tried to encourage Malakai to finish his degree and follow his own path, but had to finally admit her youngest son's greatest flaw. He liked things fast and easy. Instant gratification. He would swear he wanted to be involved with something and lose interest halfway in. Rory was constantly trying to steer him in the right direction, but Malakai was too headstrong to listen. Her oldest was compassionate, loving, resourceful, and enterprising. Her youngest was lazy, uninspired, guarded, and narcissistic. She had tried to love him. Truly tried. But how he was conceived made that a life-long battle.

"Malakai," Chrissy said, drying her hands on an apron before welcoming her son with an embrace that he did not return.

"Mother," Malakai responded, his tone curt and sharp.

"I'm making your favorite dessert. It's been so long since we've talked. I thought you'd like something special. It'll be ready soon."

Chrissy placed each ceramic ramekin, a miniature casserole dish, on the baking sheet and put them in the top portion of the stainless-steel double oven Rory installed to accommodate her passion for baking.

"Mother, I'm not here for dessert. I'm here for answers," Malakai said with no hint of emotion in his voice.

"Answers for what, my dear? Come, let's sit while this bakes." Chrissy guided Malakai over to the small table in the kitchen.

Malakai didn't sit. His hands balled into fists, then released for a moment, only to curl in again, confusing Chrissy who took a seat at the head of the table despite Malakai's resistance to do the same.

"I had a strange visitor today at the gym." Malakai ran his fingers through the shoulder length waves of his dark brown hair. Something that always looked better when cropped closer to his head. He seemed fond of the longer look, most likely, she suspected, because she didn't approve.

"Oh? Tell me more. Please, will you sit?" Chrissy pointed to the chair opposite of her. Malakai shook his head.

"His name was Anwar Futtaim," Malakai said absent of emotion, his gaze locked on her, watching the reaction closely.

"Anwar is a despicable man, Malakai," Chrissy replied, trying to keep her breathing even.

Fear stabbed into every crevice of her heart. Memories of Durabia resurfaced, almost making her slide from the chair straight to the floor. Everything Khalil Germaine did to free her from that life and now that horrid man had somehow latched onto her son. Khalil had purposely placed them in Alabama rather than in the Castle in Chicago. Futtaim had multiple business interests there and the likelihood of her running into him was too great. What possible business of Futtaim's had brought him to her doorstep?

"I want answers, Mother. He said he was my father. And that you took me from him. You said my father was killed right before we left Nadaum and made it into Durabia. What is the truth?"

She had hoped she'd never have to have this conversation. That it would remain a secret forever. She struggled as Malakai grew older, seeing the face of the man who raped her repeatedly when her husband was away for work.

*Birth control wasn't available to women in Nadaum. Every time Futtaim raped her, she'd pray that she wouldn't become pregnant. But she did. And it went unnoticed until Malakai's seventh birthday when her husband Jabir invited Anwar Futtaim to the birthday celebration. The man foolishly brought loads of presents and paid special attention to her son. The minute Jabir saw Malakai next to Anwar, he knew.*

*Jabir was never the kind and loving man she knew in Alabama. After their trip and the move to Nadaum, he was cold and treated her more like an object than a wife. When Jabir discovered the truth about his youngest son, he beat her, calling her a whore and a disgrace. She was pregnant with her daughter Mary and the abuse continued. She knew that if her baby was born alive she'd have to leave.*

*She believed Anwar sent Jabir away on purpose so his access to her would be certain. And who could she tell? Women were always blamed in these instances. Always the ones held responsible for men's lack of control and wanton lust. Some paid the ultimate price ... with their lives. No, she never told a soul, until Khalil Germaine had come to Nadaum for peace talks between warring Middle East countries. She was forced to see to his meals and needs during his stay. Futtaim even offered him the use of her body, after Khalil had inquired about the bruises that she could not hide.*

*With Futtaim departed, fully expecting her to service his new guest, she was floored when Khalil, a tall, handsome man who had a regal, almost kingly, bearing about him, immediately set her at ease. "I am going to ask you to do something that will probably not make much sense to you."*

*She was worried that he would do something debasing to her but she looked up into the most beautiful eyes she had ever seen. He wore peace as if it was a garment. But the confusion of knowing that he was associated with someone as evil as Futtaim, kept her from any hope that she would escape this night unmolested. Futtaim's business associates came in all sins and flavors, but he had never shared her this way. This was his way of exacting punishment for her refusal to lie with him willingly. The power Futtaim held over her husband was an exact measure of what he wielded over her.*

*"Your two sons and daughter," Khalil said in a low tone. "Do you know where their birth papers are?"*

*She blinked to clear her vision and thoughts. "Why do you need them?"*

*"To secure the necessary documents for you to travel to Durabia with them, and then America. Out of the reach of Futtaim, who has had your husband killed."*

*One hand flew to her mouth as tears streamed down her porcelain cheeks. "My husband? Was killed?"*

*"I am afraid so," Khalil confirmed.*

*"Why would you help me," she asked, afraid to allow herself any ounce of hope.*

*"Because Nadara told me that at first she believed her brother would cause your demise. Now she fears Futtaim killed your husband because he wanted you, unencumbered."*

*Nadara, Futtaim's sister, had been the only one to show kindness since Jabir brought her from Durabia to Nadaum. But could she trust that she would put herself at risk in this manner?*

*"What about Nadara? You know they will kill her. They will know she had a hand in this."*

*"She is already waiting in the transport to Durabia," he answered. "She would not leave without you. So, you see, I am now the one at risk."*

*Chrissy shook her head. "But why would you even be friendly with him, do business, if you knew who he was and what he's capable of?"*

*Khalil locked a steely gaze on her as he said, "Sometimes you have to wallow in the darkness to help others crawl to the light."*

* * *

"Malakai, you don't understand. Anwar raped me. He took advantage of me when he sent your father away for work."

Pacing the room, Malakai refused to look at his mother. His real father…a rapist? *That* he wouldn't believe a man with that much money would have to force himself on anyone.

"Why should I believe anything you say? You have been lying to me my entire life," Malakai yelled. "You will pay for this. Rory's father didn't want me, but my father did. You took me, and then lied to me about the fact he existed. He's rich and I would have lived in the lap of luxury."

He stormed out of the kitchen, leaving her to shed silent tears at the table.

# Chapter 15

Morning came fast after a few hours of broken sleep. Meghan's bones creaked and popped as she showered the sleep away, put on her favorite gray leggings and Woodstock 5K t-shirt, then laced up her running shoes.

Sitting down to eat a light breakfast of banana oatmeal and green tea, Meghan picked up her phone and found that not only was it almost dead, but she'd also missed several phone calls, two from Mama Ann and Mama Tee. She had to charge a bit before listening to the frantic message.

"Sweetnin'," Mama Ann said, her voice trembling on the voicemail. "Give me a call back. I got a call from Chief Carrolton, and he has me a little shook up."

"I'll be picking you up at seven o'clock for the Gala, Meghan. Be ready," Sally informed her on the next message.

"Don't worry about it." Meghan texted her reply. "I've have a few errands to run so I'll drive myself. I'll see you there. Thank you."

"You're in luck, I just had a cancellation for 1:00. It's all yours," read a text from Angela, Meghan's friend and hair stylist. She forgot she'd texted her last night after her bath.

Meghan texted Mama Ann. *Everything is fine. Just woke up, going out for a run, will call you when I get back.*

She headed towards the Vulcan Trail; her favorite place to run in the morning because it was less crowded and a lot quieter. The trail was about one mile away from her apartment, and she hoped to get at least five miles in before returning home. She made mental notes of what needed to happen when she returned. First, a call to Mama Ann, then rummaging through the closet to figure out what she was going to wear to the Gala tonight to best make an impression on folks she'd later hit up for fundraisers for JB.

Meghan was adding the final things to her mental list as she rounded the corner on the street that led to the trail. She glanced up from her sneakers and noticed a rusty red pick-up truck with a Confederate flag.

She froze in her tracks. Two tall, skinny men were sitting on the bed of the truck at the entrance to the trail, smoking and drinking, and a third man sat behind the wheel.

They weren't facing her, so they didn't know she was approaching. Meghan swept aside the dizzy feeling trying to make its way in and calculated her next move. She surveyed the area, looking for anywhere she could hide while she figured out what to do.

A silver Toyota Sienna was parked at the trailhead, and she quietly slipped behind it, leaning up against the side of the van and sliding down, heart racing as she wiped the sweat from her brow. She reached for her phone to call Chief Carrolton, then remembered that she had left it at home on the charger.

*Stupid*!

Inhaling a deep breath, Meghan counted to three and dashed off in the direction of her apartment. She made it to the end of the street before she heard, "There she is. Get her!"

Meghan ran fast, but not fast enough to keep the speeding rust bucket from catching up to her. She cut between houses, hoping she didn't run into any neighborhood dogs, or ruin any flower beds. She wove in and out of yards and stopped momentarily when she thought she'd lost them.

Catching her breath, she bent over, putting her hands on her knees to hold herself steady and inhale a stream of air.

Then she heard the rumble of the truck again.

"Bitch, we see you," the men yelled. "Stop!"

Meghan took off, this time cutting through yards that led to the back end of her cul-de-sac.

"Follow her to that goddamn apartment."

Meghan hit her stride and made it through the yard. Cruisers were parked in the turnaround. She almost passed out with relief.

Running up to a vehicle, she barely slowed down enough to avoid crashing into it.

"They're coming," Meghan told the officer, slamming a hand on the window to snap his attention away from the woman strolling past wearing a skirt so short she might as well have nothing on. "They're coming, please help!"

"Stand down, ma'am," warned the stocky officer, as he got out of his car.

The truck came barreling through the stop sign, screeching to a halt in front of Meghan's building.

"Stay here." The officer slid behind the wheel and peeled up until he was on the bumper of the truck. "Get out of the truck with your hands up," he demanded over his vehicle's microphone.

Neither of the men complied. Instead, they sped off. The officer followed them as he put the radio to his mouth, evidently calling for backup.

Meghan limped back to her apartment, hoping she was safe as the assailants were being chased by law enforcement. She was thankful for the quick action by the police.

Sue Ellyn stood outside in her housecoat, this time magenta satin, with her hands on her hips.

"What in God's name?" she asked with a hand to her forehead as if she were saluting Meghan. "Are you okay, honey?"

Meghan shook her head and tried to wrap her lips around a few words. Nothing would come.

"Bless your heart, dear," the old woman said, guiding Meghan to the threshold of her apartment. "I saw it all. Let's get you inside."

Meghan mulled over the fact that the note on her door and the untimely appearances of those men were directed at her for some strange reason. But why?

"Thank you so much," Meghan said, leaning against the wall next to her door. "I'm all right. I think I have it from here." She made a mental note to never leave the house without her phone again. "I'm going to go call the Chief now."

"Okay young lady. But when things settle down, we're going to have to talk."

Meghan rushed into her apartment, closed and locked the door, then picked up her phone.

*"Meghan, are you back yet?"* A text from Mama Ann read.

A missed call from the chief only a couple of minutes ago. A missed call from Sally.

Meghan didn't even know where to start. She responded to Mama Ann. *"I'll call you in an hour."* She dialed the chief who didn't even allow the phone to ring all the way before he said, "Meghan are you okay?"

"I don't know. They scared me a little," Meghan replied, lifting her living area curtains to peer out of the window. "No telling what they would have done to me out on that trail."

"I understand. Unfortunately, we didn't catch them. Stay where you are; I'm coming over. And for God's sake, call Andrea before she tears me a new asshole."

"Yes sir." Meghan plopped on her couch and braced herself for what she was going to hear on the other end of the line.

"Meghan Alicia Turner," Mama Ann scolded and for a moment Meghan was more afraid of her than those men. "What in God's name are you trying to do to me? Bless your ever-loving heart. What in the hell is going on over there?"

"I don't know, Mama Ann," Meghan responded, and that was the absolute truth. "I don't know. But I'm okay. The chief is coming over now."

"The hell he is. I'll beat him there, you watch." She disconnected the call before Meghan could protest. Her driving was Indy 500 worthy. Probably the main reason she was so tight with the chief. No tickets.

The next thirty minutes were a flurry of activity. First, *Angels Watching Over Me*, a little Gospel music to change the fearful vibe, then clearing the towels from the bathtub fiasco last night, followed by tidying up for all the people who were headed to her house. The officer who pursued the Bradland Boys came to the door, followed by Chief, with Andrea right behind him. "God damnit, how did he get here first?" she said.

Chief and Meghan both laughed, knowing Mama Ann had come from the other side of the city and didn't stand a chance against a cruiser with sirens blaring.

Meghan silently whispered a prayer of thanksgiving that Mama Ann didn't get pulled over or cause a wreck as fast as she had to be going to make it to Meghan's apartment in Homewood so quickly.

"Please everyone, find a spot." Meghan pushed herself up to sit on the breakfast counter as there were no more open seats. Mama Ann settled on the couch in the space next to the chief, and the responding officer chose to stand. "This apartment isn't set up for so much company."

"What's going on?" Mama Ann demanded.

"Calm down, Andrea," the chief warned as he put his hand on her knee to comfort her. "Officer Michaels, can you tell us what you know?"

"Well, the plates are registered to John Gregory. He's a known meth dealer who just got out of prison. We don't know if he was in the vehicle or who the other two might have been." He held up a photograph from a line-up on his Samsung Galaxy smartphone. "Miss Meghan, do you know this man?"

Meghan shook her head. "No, sir. What could he want with me? I don't understand why this is happening. I—"

"Chief, we're going to talk to the St. Clair County Sheriff's Department and have them go out to Bradland," Officer Michaels said. "We know Richards ain't gonna do nothing 'bout this."

"That sounds like a good plan," the chief conceded. "Get to it. I'm going to stay here with these ladies for a while."

"Yes, sir." Officer Michaels left the apartment with a tip of his hat.

"Meghan, is there anything going on at work that could have people wanting to come after you?"

Meghan sighed, wondering if she should say anything about Candace and the other missing women. That's the only thing she could think of. "I help women from all over the state who are guests of the Alabama penal system. I only know why they are in, but nothing else about them."

Meghan's gaze bounced between Chief and Mama Ann. They both knew Candace and her family, and from their expressions they could tell she was holding something back. "Candace went missing from her group home this week."

"What in the hell do you mean … *missing*?" Andrea piped in, the deep crease between her eyebrows indicating her level of frustration. "She wouldn't just walk out. That's a ticket straight back to Tutwiler."

Chief motioned for Mama Ann to quiet down. "Tell me more about this, Meghan. How is she missing? Are you sure she wasn't moved to one of your other homes? Or decided to call it quits? Have you talked to her family?"

Meghan put her focus on the round rug at the base of her breakfast counter. She dangled her feet above the circle patterns before looking back up at Mama Ann and the Chief. "That's not what happened. She never would've left because she knows she would never get her kids back." Meghan rubbed her palms against her thighs. "And another thing; her name doesn't come up in the system anymore. It's like she never existed."

Chief's bushy eyebrows drew in.

"And there are more women," she added. "They all fit a certain profile, except for Candace. I'm supposed to talk with this man from some type of castle organization in Chicago. His name is Rory Tannous, and he's supposed to help us. But I'm so scared. Who is he? Why is this happening?"

Meghan closed her eyes, trying to find a sense of calm. The events of the last week had finally caught up with her. The uncertainty of it all was overwhelming.

The chief stood and invited Meghan to come closer. "Bring it in," he whispered before engulfing her and Mama Ann in a bear hug. "You're going to be okay. We won't let anything happen to you. "I'll go back to the station and run a background check on this Rory person. I'll let you know if you're going to be in good hands."

# Chapter 16

Rory pushed the button to start the car, opened the windows and sunroof, and told the car to play his Spotify playlist. First song on deck …Alice DJ's *Better off Alone*.

Putting the car into gear, he sped out of the parking lot towards his next destination.

After a trip to the cleaners, he planned to walk over to McCallister's for lunch. It had been a long time since he'd had a good sandwich, and he was craving their black angus club and giant spuds ever since he's made it back on American soil. Then he'd take the time to reflect on all of the research he'd done on Meghan Turner.

As Rory pulled out onto Lakeshore Drive, his phone rang.

"Daron Kincaid," the robotic voice announced.

"Answer," Rory commanded. "Daron, what's going on?"

"What can I say, it's a great day to be a King," Daron stated.

"Or a Knight," Rory shot back.

"How are you doing?" asked Daron.

"No complaints," Rory replied. "I'm looking forward to attending the gala tonight. First big event since being home."

"Listen, I've got some intel for you on your assignment. I spoke with my contact, Lisa, who gave me the lead on the situation, and provided a little more information. She wants you to hear it directly from Meghan and her partner, Sally."

"So three women head up the organization?" asked Rory.

"No, Sally is Lisa's romantic partner. Keep up."

"Dude, you just tossed out three whole names into the mix," Rory countered, making a turn onto Cahaba Heights Road. "You said partner, I'm just trying to make sure I have the details right."

Daron chuckled and said, "Sally reported that there are women missing from Tutwiler prison and the transitional homes associated with Meghan's non-profit. Lisa thinks it has something to do with this organization. The program helps incarcerated women get out of prison and they're going missing before they get that chance."

Rory continued listening to Daron who was speaking quickly and sounded like he was in a subway station.

"Listen, I don't know what any of this means, but it sounds like this woman is in trouble. She'll be at the gala event with Sally and Lisa. Meghan has a connection with Luis Fry, but I don't know the history just yet. Keep your eyes and ears open until we know more about what's going on here."

Rory glanced in his rearview mirror. "You got it boss," he said, pulling off to the side to allow a series of emergency vehicles to pass. "I'll see you tonight."

Thoughts about Meghan swirled in Rory's mind. He was intrigued by her organization that had a goal of impacting those who needed it most. He was passionate about helping underprivileged, abused, and trafficked women, especially after what his mother went through with her marriage that landed her in Nadaum. After much contemplation, he decided that he would research Meghan's organization after he ran a few errands.

Rory stopped at the dry cleaners to pick-up his tuxedo. Malakai was supposed to bring it home for him, but he was nowhere to be found and unreachable.

"Rory Tannous," a familiar voice exclaimed causing Rory to look up. He put his focus on the face of Luis, who was grinning like they were long lost friends.

Rory reluctantly shook Luis's outstretched hand, and before he could put some distance between them, the man had pulled him in for a hug. "What a surprise. I didn't think I'd have the pleasure of seeing your ugly mug until tonight."

"Seems to be a popular spot," Rory said, ignoring the slight as two men walked around them, also carrying tuxes sheathed in dry cleaner plastic.

"How've you been?"

Rory studied Luis's face before answering. He had the nerve to call him ugly when the man looked as though he'd had a rough night. Dark circles marred his caramel skin, which was more pallid than normal. His lips were dry and his breath smelled like he'd had bourbon for breakfast.

"I'm good," Rory responded, stepping away to get Luis out of his personal space and adjusting his clothes. "As a matter of fact, I'm great. What's up with you? You look like hell warmed over and baked twice."

Luis gave a hearty laughed, as if what Rory said was hysterical. "Hermano," he said exaggerating the *r*. "The girls last night at Walker's party were hot. Insane, man." He gestured at his groin area like a rapper on stage instead of a man who'd pulled himself up from meager beginnings and now had political aspirations for a seat in Congress. "Pretty little Black girls had my big guy going all night. It hurts to walk, man. You should've been there."

Rory looked at him, trying to keep a straight face at the words as well as the delivery—from proper eloquent English to common language. What stood out most was … *Girls, not women.* That certainly wasn't his scene, and he didn't figure it would be for a prominent judge like Abdul Walker or Luis either. Maybe the Castle had even more cause for concern. *Girls, not women.*

"Sounds like you had a good time."

"Oh yeah," Luis said as he shifted away from the front of the door. "Make sure you're ready for the after party. I don't know if I've got any left in me, so it's time to share the chocolate love." Luis winked and his lips lifted in a sly smile. "If you know what I mean."

The salaciousness of the invitation along with the fact that Malakai was mixed up in the madness made Rory's blood boil. "I'll keep that in mind. Listen, I have to get my tux. So, I'll see you tonight."

"Hell yeah," Luis shouted as if Rory was a distance away instead of only a few feet.

Rory held his composure, despite his disgust at having to be enveloped in yet another hug and a handshake before the man sauntered off in the direction of the enclosed parking garage for the shops.

Rory wanted nothing to do with Luis' after party, but thought he might have to check it out to confirm his suspicions. One quick call to Daron was necessary to see if he knew what these parties were all about and if it was a cover for something else. Then he'd make the determination on how much to share with his King brothers after he found out what was going on with Meghan Turner.

# Chapter 17

Arriving at Rossman Bridge Resort, Meghan parked her car, stepped out and locked the doors.

"Damn," she snapped, then, surveyed the area to see who would chastise her poor manners, she unlocked her car to retrieve her phone and purse and proceeded to a pathway leading to a set of gold and glass revolving doors. In her haste, Meghan, navigating in a brand-new pair of high heels, missed her footing onto the curb and took a tumble so hard she went ass-over-head in pure slapstick comedy style.

Her phone slid across the pebble stone paved sidewalk, her purse emptied out around her, and her knee glistened with bright red blood.

*Of course I fell. Why not? With the way this day was shaping up I should've expected it.*

The meeting between Meghan, Mama Ann, and the chief lasted far into the afternoon. Much longer than she had anticipated as Chief Carrolton had to calm Sue Ellyn's fears. The last thing Meghan needed to worry about was being kicked out of her home because of all the drama.

Meghan didn't have time to break down. Tonight was important. Maybe she would find out why the Bradland Boys chased her down this morning. Then again, she should probably leave that to the trusty Homewood PD.

As she waved away offers of help from several people who rushed forward to assist, and made an attempt to collect the contents of her bag, she heard a male voice say, "I'll call you right back." Then a car door opened before closing a few moments later.

Meghan vowed not to look up as she Army crawled around, all grace and modesty lost at this point. Unfortunately, she was showing the world her neon green panties with "bottoms-up" decorating her derriere in pink glitter box letters before she could pull her dress back down. She might have to dress up on the outside, but kept it cute and comfortable underneath. At the moment, she regretted not going with the floor length gown that didn't have the almost-up-to-Heaven spilt like the one she had on. At least her "bottom" would have been covered.

She heard the man's footsteps approaching as he cleared his throat.

"Are you okay, ma'am?" He didn't quite have a Southern accent, but a little twang touched his sexy voice. Deciding to embrace the hot mess she'd made of herself, she looked up and laughed at the first aid kit in his hands.

"Yes, thank you. I'm good," Meghan assured, her gaze locked on the man she could only believe was an angel in disguise. "Just working on my grace and bruised ego over here."

In an expertly tailored tuxedo, the man squatted down in perfect form with very little effort, making it easy to hold Meghan's gaze. He smiled with what seemed to be genuine warmth.

"Pardon my intrusion, but it doesn't look like you're okay. You're bleeding and your belongings are—" the man scanned the space area around her. "Well, they are everywhere. Allow me to help you."

People dressed in sequined ball gowns and expensive suits swelled around them, giving curious glances.

"Nothing here to see, people," he said over his shoulder.

"Let's keep it moving."

People heeded his advice and she was grateful he had said something to allow her to have a tiny bit of dignity.

A nervous laugh escaped Meghan as she moved from her position on her knees to sit, folding her legs. He used hand sanitizer to clean his hands before stroking the antiseptic wipes over her brand new addition to her skin family. He placed a dap of antiseptic cream on the spot, and she was feeling no pain. She wasn't in a position to say no at this point, with her life spread all over the walkway.

Meghan looked up at the man who was offering to help in her distressed state. From where she sat, she didn't think he was too much taller than her five-feet-eight. He had expertly styled thick black hair and a five o'clock shadow that was the perfect accent to his sharp chiseled facial features. His skin held a light bronze glow as though he'd recently vacationed on a sunny beach. He looked like he just walked off of the latest People's Sexiest Man Alive magazine cover.

She conceded, tucked her pride aside, and allowed this dangerously handsome man to assist. Then maybe he'd go away so she could put herself back together and enjoy some parts of the gala tonight.

"So you just happen to have one of these in the car?"

"Don't you? I always like to be prepared."

"I see you're one of those Boy Scout types."

He favored her with a megawatt smile and said, "No, I couldn't be considered one of those. Sometimes I liked to get a little down and dirty."

"Boy Scouts can do that too," she countered as he placed a large band-aid over her new sore spot. His touch was smooth, gentle, and it took every effort not to take his hand and let it slide the rest of the way up her thigh.

His lips quirked as if he were holding back his true thoughts. "I'm a little afraid of the thought that just ran through your mind," she said, and the husky tone of her voice was almost unrecognizable. *Where the hell did that come from?*

She picked up the scattered belongings that were within her reach.

"You should be," he countered with a wink.

"And not a humble bone in his body."

"Humble? What's that?"

Meghan laughed and he joined in.

"Thank you, sir." Meghan's breath hitched as he handed her the small pile of her belongings. His almond shaped, deep blue eyes were soft and smiling under a pair of dark framed glasses that fit his face perfectly. Meghan always had a thing for a man with a goatee and five o'clock shadow and he wore it well. She didn't think it was fair that a man could simply put on a pair of fitted pants, simple white shirt, bow-tie and sexy as sin black patent leather shoes shined to perfection, and look that good with so little effort. He smelled like the ocean with a dash of citrus—fresh and crisp.

"Allow me to help you up, ma'am," the man said in a tone that didn't allow for protest, but she did anyway.

"No, I'm—" Meghan protested as she fumbled with dropping the stray items in her purse.

"Please, I insist. You're not the first person to have a bad day, you know. I'm Rory, by the way. Please, take my hand."

Meghan looked up at him, and in her haze, tried to remember what she should say next. Her name, yes, her name. "I'm Meghan," she said, situating her collected items in her purse.

Meghan accepted his hand and gracious offer, holding his gaze, taking note of the softness of his touch, a touch that stole her next breath.

Rory grasped Meghan's forearm and helped her to her feet where they stood face to face, gazing into each other's eyes, neither saying a word.

"Oh … um… thanks, Rory." Meghan giggled like a schoolgirl as heat rushed to her cheeks. The embarrassment hit her all the same. "Your name has a certain flow to it."

The corners of his lips turned up, his grin growing wider the longer he stared at Meghan. "Really? Rory is a common enough name in these parts. This area is the Irish capital of the state of Alabama."

"So, you're Irish?"

"Only when I drink," he quipped. "Isn't everyone on March 17th?"

Meghan shook her head as if to bring herself back to earth. "Well, thank you so much for your help," she said, looking over his shoulder to the entrance where Sally's head was peeking out, watching the scene unfold. "I hope I didn't hold you up from your call."

"No, you didn't," Rory replied. "You simply added to the adventure."

Meghan averted her gaze as she twirled a lock of hair around a finger.

"Thanks again," Meghan said, pointing toward the building. "I have to go in. I'm meeting someone here."

"If you give me a moment, I'll walk you in," he said.

"My friend is waiting at the door," she said, pulling her phone out to check the time.

Rory shifted his focus to the entrance to find Sally and Lisa giving him a Miss America wave.

"Yes, of course. It was my pleasure to assist." Rory pulled a cell from his pants pocket and glanced at the screen. "Hopefully, the rest of the event will go a lot smoother."

"I'll certainly hope so," Meghan assured, pulling her purse strap onto her shoulder. "Have a good rest of your day as well."

Meghan, finding what little dignity she didn't leave on the ground, held her head high as she sauntered towards the building. As she made it to the entry way, she flashed a smile over her shoulder, discovering he was watching her every move.

# Chapter 18

As Rory walked back to his BMW to stash his sunglasses, he couldn't stop thinking of the scene that just played out. That poor woman was a beautiful mess. Her purple dress did nothing to hide her more intimate apparel that clearly was an afterthought for the evening. Her auburn hair was piled on top of her head in what looked like an attempt at an elegant updo. Her pale skin made those freckles stand out even though her cheeks were flushed, enhancing her beautiful blue eyes. He smiled as he thought of her name. *Meghan.*

That's when it hit him. He took his phone out of his pocket and pulled up the photo that Daron had sent him.

*No, it can't be.* He swapped out the black rimmed glasses for his favorite prescription silver Ray Ban aviators, and looked toward the banquet entrance to see if he could catch a glimpse of her again. The swarm of people lined up to enter prevented him from confirming his suspicions.

"*She* can't be *that Meghan*," he sighed as he smoothed out his goatee realizing she looked even better in person than she had on his phone screen —despite her tumble and obvious discomfort.

*What are the odds of that?* But he couldn't get the sight of her unconventional underwear from his mind. *Bottoms up indeed*, he thought with a chuckle.

Rory adjusted his collar as heat rushed to his neck remembering her touch—soft, gentle, and hot. This Meghan, in person, stirred feelings that were unfamiliar to Rory. It had been a long time since he felt a connection with any woman. She was earthy, warm and sexy. Seems like she had been so flustered she didn't realize who he was.

Earlier at lunch, Rory scrolled through the information Daron had sent him about Meghan's professional history and the services offered by The Journey Beyond.

Since obtaining her law degree, her life to this non-profit so that the women she served could live their lives free with the privileges she was born with.

"A 'woke' White woman," Rory said with an appreciative nod. This world could use more of them. The same people who put laws and created obstacles for people of color also had no love for women—White or otherwise. Except when they were in their bed or in the delivery room.

That's the main reason being a member of The Castle appealed to Rory so much. Men, from different ethnic backgrounds, were actually pulling to change things on a global level. Definitely a far cry from the "lip service" politicians were giving these days.

While the BLM movement was picking up steam because of the outlandish disregard for human life, it put White people like Meghan and even Rory in a tough position having to explain their "whys" to people in their family, and also reaffirm that they were on the side of justice to people of color.

People tended to forget that some Whites had been involved on the front lines in opposing societal norms for as long as someone had as voice to speak out against the wrongs committed against the oppressed. Civil Rights had any number of women like Viola Liuzzo, Sarah and Angelina Grimke who also risked their lives to see justice for all. Some of them landed in an early grave.

Evidently, with Meghan's efforts being focused more on marginalized women of color, someone wasn't taking it too well. How dare she help Black and Brown women have a better handle on life? That would certainly put her at risk for the ire of men like the Bradland Boys and even some top-level politicians. Keeping things the same worked well for people already in power. They aimed to do everything possible to make sure change was minimal even for their own women and still always in their own favor.

Rory took some time to study the picture again and thought of the woman whose image was nothing short of amazing and aptly matched her purpose. That was sexy as hell. Purpose. Meaning. Mission.

There were parts of the state that were still very segregated. Black and Brown people were targeted when they crossed the line. Verbally attacked daily. At work and in school. Especially in the area he lived in.

Even the day he first brought Marcus and James hoping to convince them to move their families in with him since he would spend so much time abroad, they were pulled over by the trusted police force the minute they crossed over into Brook Haven.

They came in James' old tan Nissan Quest Van. Admittedly, it had seen better days. A couple of the doors had been replaced from junk yard parts so the colors didn't match, and the tires were near bald. It didn't fit the aesthetics of the neighborhood. The two men, whose families had owned farmland for decades, lost everything when they went up against a corporation whose whole plan was to take down individuals who were still working their own land, and sell it to those who would use their genetically modified seeds. They were pulled out of the car, illegally searched, handcuffed, and forced to sit on the curb on display so the whole town knew they didn't belong.

Neveah managed to text Rory before they cuffed her. Rory and Malakai arrived in separate cars, rushed to the intersection where seven cruisers were now on the scene. Rory, a well-known resident of Brook Haven for the work he did in developing properties in Birmingham, immediately called his friend, a captain on the force. He demanded the release of his friends who had done nothing wrong.

The cops didn't like it, but they complied when their lieutenant had given the order, not without force and openly spoken racist comments. Rory led the way with Malakai pulling up the rear so the van traveled, escorted, the rest of the way to the estate.

James and Marcus didn't want to move their families in. They didn't ever want to return to Brook Haven again. Rory insisted and bought each of them vehicles, despite much opposition.

Rory remembered the outrage of his neighbors when those new families moved in to care for his property. Even though the neighbors lived at least a quarter of a mile apart from each other, his team was still harassed whenever they pulled onto the road leading to his estate. But James and Marcus weathered the storm because their children and wives were flourishing, and they were amassing enough money to buy their own homes and not be saddled with the debt that had come with the loss. And while things hadn't been easy in the neighborhood, they were at least settled.

So if Meghan Turner was in trouble, considering her line of work, he wouldn't be surprised. He still wasn't sure where Luis Fry fit into all of this, but he was determined to find out. And though he didn't want to admit it, Rory had been both excited and a little nervous to meet Meghan tonight. If he had such a connection with her just through seeing her photo and understanding that her life's mission aligned with his, he couldn't imagine what would happen when they were finally face to face.

And then again, now he could. *Bottoms up.*

# *Chapter 19*

Candace shivered, trying not to move as she laid on the cool concrete floor of a takhzin—more like a shed. She tugged on the towel, pulling it over her arms, then jerking the thin fabric to cover her feet. Even the hot temperatures of the desert weren't warm enough to keep the chill of the ground from reaching her bones. She slowly drew her knees into her chest as, angry voices came closer to her makeshift home.

*Do not make a sound*

Emir's warning shook Candace as she overheard the men discuss the plans.

"Futtaim has more women coming tomorrow," one voice said. "Let the trainers know to be ready. They will need to be cleaned upon arrival. The plane lands at eight."

"So are we supposed to stand around and babysit the throw away?" asked another voice.

"Yes. If you can believe it, someone bought her for 1900 Riyal." The two roared a hearty laugh. "That was too much."

"Indeed." Emir's stern voice came through and his next words were painful to hear. "Futtaim might as well keep her for housework for that little money. If you," he paused as the men laughed, then added, "are done with the business of spending other people's money, you are relieved of your duties now."

"Futtaim said that we stay, and we can have a turn with her. He promised."

"How long have you worked for Futtaim and do not know he fails at every hand to keep his promises?" Emir laughed, and the sound of it rang in her ears. "He sent me to handle her because she struck one of the other wives during training."

Candace's heart raced as she comprehended what Emir said. In her flailing to escape, she gave the woman a bruise on her cheek. Her muscles stiffened as she fought the urge to release the contents of her bladder.

*He's coming to kill me.*

"Now leave," Emir demanded. "I don't need an audience today."

Candace's body trembled as she heard feet shuffling away. Her hands flew up to her mouth to hold in a scream as the door swung open.

"Shhh," Emir whispered, stepping into the cramped space. He banged on the tools and growled. Reaching across his body, he drew a belt from his waist and snapped it in the air. "Stop your crying. You will be broken from your disrespectful ways." He signaled his hand and it took a second to understand what he meant. She gave a sharp cry that echoed in the space. Emir glanced over his shoulder and nodded.

Candace flinched and scrambled to keep the cloth from exposing her nakedness with all of Emir's theatrics. She heaved, trying to catch her breath.

They repeated their efforts a few more times before Emir his finger to his lips, waited several minutes, then opened the door and pulled in a bag. Kneeling in front of Candace, he took out a napkin and placed it front of her, holding a tender gaze.

She marveled at his movements as he carefully emptied the contents of the sack.

Emir reached in and pulled out a small loaf of bread, a few pieces of grilled chicken, some fruit, and a bottle of water.

Candace's eyes widened at the gift. "Thank you," she whispered around a mouthful of the bread. "Why are you being so kind to me?"

"You need to be well when they come for you."

"Rescued?" She dared to let a smidgen of hope shine through.

"Yes, we have special forces coming to assist."

"What about the others?" Candace asked. "The women who were brought in with me?"

Emir walked to the door of the takhzin and looked out before glancing at her over his shoulder. "We are handling one situation at a time," Emir stated. "I must apologize as this may be your only meal today."

Candace took a bite of the bread and shoved a few grapes into her mouth. "Thank you," she replied around the sweet morsels.

"I will be standing guard, but you must still be quiet. Please be patient. "When night falls, we do not want to bring attention to ourselves."

Candace filled her stomach as Emir exited the takhzin.

*Be patient? I need to get out of here before whoever bought me comes to collect.*

# Chapter 20

Meghan glared at Sally who had covered her mouth, laughing. "Don't say one word," Meghan warned through her teeth. "Not. One. Word."

Sally closed her mouth, then pretended to pull a zipper across her lips, and formed a neutral expression. All of which lasted exactly three seconds before she burst out laughing and Lisa joined her.

"To hell with the both of y'all," Meghan snapped and stormed past them on her way to the restroom to pull the rest of herself together.

"But he *was* fine," Sally yelled after her.

Meghan walked out several minutes later to find the two friends waiting at the entrance of the foyer leading to the ballroom. She was shocked at how well Sally and Lisa cleaned up. Both were wearing coordinating pant suits. Sally even had on heels that gave her a good deal of height to match Lisa's stature. Lisa clearly was in charge of wardrobe for the evening. Because if Sally had a say, they would have shown up wearing V-neck white t-shirts and tan Adidas warm-up pants with white superstar shoes.

"Everything is white and gold," Sally said, exasperated by the outlandish displays of Middle Eastern decor. "I thought this was for a non-profit. How can they afford this?"

The DJ was playing traditional Egyptian and Middle Eastern music.

Red and gold silk ribbons draped the performance stage as lights moved around the room to the cadence of the music. A woman in flowing blue and green chiffon fabrics entered the area twirling batons alight with fire on both ends. Belly dancers took to the floor, entertaining the guests with hip rolls and swaying arms. Ropes and satin garlands hung from the ceiling where beautiful women were spinning like stars in orbit. Handsome men wearing kaftans served drinks made to order at the bars in each corner of the hall. Ornate boxes with gold W's for Wellbound on the face for the guests to leave cash donations in lieu of tips.

"These tables are beautiful," Lisa said, waving a manicured hand towards the banquet spread of fresh vegetables, hummus and naan along with other Middle Eastern fare.

"It feels like we've stepped through the door into a different country," Meghan said, admiring the bright costumes worn by the dancers and performers.

Meghan felt like she had travelled into a dream. She only wished JB could produce such a spectacle. She had always felt every dime should go into programs and salaries. Evidently, from the amount of people attending the gala, it took money to bring in more money.

After taking in the whole scene, Meghan, Sally and Lisa walked in to meet the greeter who wore a blue Jacquard Sherwani with gold pants, standing at a gold podium with a book Meghan assumed were filled with the guest's names.

"Good evening, ladies," the greeter said, nodding with a warm smile. "Your names please?"

"Meghan Turner," she informed him.

"Lisa Montoya and Sally Decker," Lisa announced.

Once again, he nodded and raised his hand to call someone to come to the podium. A woman with black hair that flowed flawlessly down to her calves sauntered to the podium.

"Table 216 for the ladies, please."

"Yes sir," she replied. "Please, follow me this way."

Arriving at the table situated near the dance floor, Meghan recognized several of the guests who were already seated. One was Jim Wheeler, an assistant DA who handled special crimes, along with his wife. He was a striking man with a well-fitting tux of deep maroon with a gold tie and gold shoes. He really took the suggested wardrobe seriously. More seriously than his wife Olivia who wore a simple black dress and red bottomed black stilettos. The other was Jessica Fabian, a legal aid who worked in the courthouse, running errands for the DA's office. One of the last guests was her former employer, Scott Willingham, who openly glared at her as if she'd stolen his wife. Something his predecessor had managed, which probably still stung since the man was fifteen years older.

The hostess pulled out the chairs where Meghan, Sally, and Lisa were to be seated. She reached over them and poured wine into each of the glasses situated in front of the women.

"Dinner will be served at eight. Please enjoy the hors d'oeuvres. Have a marvelous evening," she said with a Vanna White wave, mentioning where everything was stationed before returning to the next set of guests standing near the host.

Banter about government and state legislation was the topic of conversation of the table, but Meghan wasn't in the mood to talk politics and barely heard them over the noise throughout the hall. The place was a special kind of sensory overload for a woman who preferred the simpler pleasures in life.

Meghan's thoughts panned to the man who had helped her up from the ground like some type of Knight rescuing a damsel in distress. Then another thought came to mind and her pulse took an uptick at the mere thought of meeting Rory Tannous. She kicked herself for not asking her Knight's last name, but the odds of another Rory being in attendance was pretty good. He was right, while most Irish Americans were concentrated in the northeast, Cullman County, Alabama was considered the Irish capital, with more than twelve percent of the population claiming Irish heritage.

Her gaze roamed the crowded space as she took a sip of wine and scanned for the man who was "prepared for any situation".

"Are you okay?" Sally asked, searching Meghan's face. "You zoned out for a second."

"I'm fine. Just taking in the scenery," Meghan explained, tipping the glass to her lips. "Can you believe this event? We could learn a few things for JB. Maybe we need to go a little bigger next time."

Tingles zipped up her arm as she felt someone touch her, breaking her from the mission to find Rory, and also from wondering when Sally's guest would show up. Sally motioned behind her before Lisa left her seat and walked over to the newcomer and shook his hand.

"You must be Rory," Lisa said with a foxy grin, looking a bit starry-eyed, which struck Meghan as strange considering she preferred women.

Meghan's knees nearly buckled as she met with an intense ocean blue gaze. A smile split her face as embarrassment tried to creep in. Her thoughts became wayward—any words she had were lost on her tongue. Heat rushed to her cheeks and ears as she considered looking away. However, she was enjoying the view a little too much and swimming in the depths of the possibilities.

"I'm Lisa," said the voice that broke Meghan's trance. "Daron said he was bringing you in to help with our … issues. This is my partner Sally, and this is Meghan. She runs the non-profit The Journey Beyond."

Rory gave Sally and Lisa's hands a shake. He smiled as his gaze first swept across her face, then lowered until he landed on that telltale Band-Aid on her left knee.

Meghan was still unable to find anything to say as she stared in his eyes after admiring the sight of him.

"Yes, Meghan," he said bridging the silence as he leaned in to capture her hand in his. He responded in a warm tenor voice, that had a decidedly sensual vibe. "Pleased to officially meet you. Just so you know, neon green is now my favorite color."

Meghan overcame her shock, extracted her hands from his, and lifted the wineglass in a mock salute. "Bottoms up."

Rory tossed his head back and laughed as Meghan joined in.

Sally and Lisa shared a questioning glance then put their focus back on Rory and Meghan.

"Inside joke," Meghan told them as the corners of Sally's mouth twitched at the same time a penciled eyebrow shot up on Lisa's forehead.

Meghan nodded, giving herself that inside pep talk so she wouldn't make an absolute fool of herself. *Get it together. You are a successful, strong, professional woman. Your life's goal is to improve the lives of other women. You will not allow yourself to be this affected by any man, especially not this one.*

She drew in a deep breath, and released it finally having her thoughts together. "It's good to see you in a more …vertical way."

"I don't know," he teased. "Horizontal was working quite well. I'm glad you were the victor in that fight. I love a woman who knows how to make an awesome comeback." He extended his hand as if this was their first-time meeting.

Meghan took in the intensity of his gaze and the admiration in his tone. She braced herself against the unexpected sparks igniting while taking his hand for a much different reason this time. She shook it with confidence, pleased with herself for not giving away that there were butterflies that had a launch pad in her belly.

* * *

Rory relished the feel of her hand in his yet another time. Her skin was silky to the touch. Her pulse had picked up speed and he realized that she was just as affected as he was.

He decided as a teen to never marry—he never wanted to be in a relationship after watching his mother's abuse. Though he saw his father's features when he looked in the mirror, he also caught a glimpse of his mother's soulful, yet somber eyes. It's not that Rory didn't love women. He adored them; their strength, their resilience, their beauty; but the fear of becoming like his father crippled his thoughts of ever being in love.

His hope was shot the second Meghan Turner squared her shoulders, lifted her chin to meet his gaze head on, then slid her hand into his.

Electricity coursed through his body the moment her fingers flexed in his. She had made subtle changes since their encounter; her auburn hair was now pulled up in an elegant soft style, with strands falling on each side, lightly curled and framing her heart shaped face. Her blue eyes glistened under the glow of chandelier lights hanging over their table. Rory was all too prepared to help in any way he could, but would have to set some internal boundaries early on to keep things professional and to accomplish their yet to be determined mission.

"Lisa," Rory said, shifting his gaze away from Meghan. "Shall we find somewhere more private to catch up? Reno says 'hi', by the way."

*"They don't know what's going on," Reno informed Rory after Meghan left in him the parking lot. "They think Meghan might be targeted as well and suspect her relationship with Candace might be the reason. She has received threats at home. There was a suspicious note left on her door and she was chased down by some locals when she was out on a jog this morning. Lisa is scared for the women who are missing, and for Meghan. Make sure they're safe."*

"I'll have to call Mr. DeLuca and thank him for sending someone so handsome," Lisa said, sounding more friendly than she should, considering the reason for their meeting. "I like the way the Kings work. Fast and efficient."

"For crying out loud," Sally said with hint of disdain as she watched Lisa fawn over Rory. "Dinner will be served in just a few minutes. Maybe we should wait?"

Lisa snapped a look at Sally, then Sally shot a glance Meghan. "Fine, we'll wait," they said in unison, then looked at each other and chuckled.

"Sounds like a plan." Rory walked around the table pulling the chairs out for each of the women under the curious gazes of the other two men who remained next to their wives. Since neither one of them seemed inclined to make pleasantries, Rory introduced himself. The hostess had already filled his wine glass while he was chatting with the women, so he took a hearty sip and settled into the space directly next to the woman whose whole vibe shouted, "this is who I am, take me or leave me."

Something within him said taking her would be the best thing to happen in his love life—as sparse as it had been.

"Meghan, tell me why you started The Journey Beyond," he said figuring that if they got right to business, he could distract himself from the fact that the blood coursing through his veins was going in the wrong direction.

Meghan's face lit up as she adjusted her posture, her hands folded tightly in front of her on the table, as if she were trying to hold them back from carrying the conversation all by themselves. She wore a soft, yet serious expression as she shared with him, the intricate details about The Journey Beyond program, then said, "It started after I became disgusted by what I saw happening in our criminal justice system. The DA's office was corrupt." Her head tilted as though mulling something over. "Still is, if you want my honest opinion. Back then though, before Luis was the lead prosecutor, it was worse."

The men at the table shifted as though uncomfortable with the direction of the discussion. Sally gave Meghan a warning glare, which she ignored.

Meghan shook her head as though acknowledging Sally's not-so-subtle concern, but she continued sharing her experience as an intern early in her law career. "This one case though, it really got to me, and I knew I had to do something better with my education." Her lips pursed as she flickered a gaze at the wineglass, almost as if she wanted to partake, but felt telling her story was more important than her own physical needs.

Rory reached over, handed her the glass and waited as she took a sip while watching him over the rim. "Thank you," she said, favoring him with a smile that made him inhale to keep steady.

"Angelica Ruiz was only fourteen when she committed her crime and had been in prison for ten years of her fifty-year sentence. She killed the man who was pimping her out and raking in money from the sordid efforts. Shot him, burned him, then ran away. She had finally had enough and cracked." Meghan paused and he could see the fire behind her eyes as she told the story. The anger, the pain—all of it was on display.

Rory remembered that case well, it had made national news along with several others with the same scenario.

"This dude has been in and out of jail and was being investigated for trafficking, yet law enforcement still had him out doing his thing." Meghan's blue orbs misted, but she took a long, slow breath to keep her composure. "They claimed they were about to make an arrest, but that was only a claim with no merits to back it up. Angelica took that burden away from them. And the DA, prosecutor, and the judge all hung her out to dry."

Rory looked down and found that her fingers had wrapped tightly around the napkin. He placed a hand over hers and gave it a reassuring squeeze as the room filled with guests who had arrived closer to dinner time than cocktail hour.

"I met her when she was at her fifth appeal hearing. I sat on the People's side with Luis Fry who was just an intern with the prosecutor at the time."

He stilled upon hearing that name.

"The way they spoke of her as if she were a piece of meat. They treated her as if her crime was premeditated, then painted her abuser as if he were the King of Birmingham." She glanced over to Lisa as a tear streaked down the woman's face, before putting her focus back on him. "It was horrifying, Rory. She got her win, and a year and a half later, Angelica became the first client of The Journey Beyond. Now, she works with Wellbound, the charity this gala is raising money for to help other women like her. That's what my program is all about. Helping women become who they were meant to be before the U-turn that slid them behind bars. Life after prison."

Rory was speechless. If it wouldn't be considered rude, he would have closed his eyes, just to feel her every word deep in his soul. The passion that came through as she shared her testimony gave him chills. Sally's eyes had glazed over as Meghan spoke, and this was more than what he'd expected when he first laid eyes on the picture Daron sent him. This was the precise moment he was certain that he had to be careful.

Meghan was the one woman that he never wanted to encounter in his lifetime.

# Chapter 21

As dinner got under way with meals in front of all of the guests, the first speaker took the podium. Looking up at the stage where a familiar voice saluted the audience, Meghan's jaw clenched.

"Good Evening guests, thank you all for attending the First Annual Break the Chains Gala, raising money for the amazing organization, The Wellbound House." His hand swept in an encompassing wave, "I am your State Prosecutor, Luis Fry, and the newest board member of this most auspicious organization."

Pausing for applause, Luis looked around the ballroom at all the attendees, then thanked their sponsors and benefactors, and all the people who played a part in putting the fundraiser together.

"I personally want to thank the Futtaim Foundation for sponsoring this gala and their generous donation of one million dollars to go towards the building of Wellbound's new safehouse for women. This money will benefit victims of human trafficking that find themselves in Alabama, give them the opportunity to rehabilitate at no expense to them, and ultimately get the training they need to reenter society and go on leading happy and healthy lives."

Luis extended his hand to Mr. Futtaim, who stood and nodded to the attendees.

"We couldn't do what we do without donations such as this, and we look forward to exceeding our fundraising goals with the support of our guests tonight."

Luis panned the audience, but his gaze locked on Maria as he said, "We have a great evening planned for you tonight. So please, enjoy your meals and get ready for the most exciting gala experience in Birmingham. Then show us some love with your plastic."

He winked and left the podium to return to his seat next to Maria Sanchez whose bodycon style dress was like painted liquid gold against her tan complexion.

* * *

Maria was sight to behold, despite her stoic appearance. Almond-shaped, dark brown eyes told a painful story of why she was present at The Wellbound fundraiser. Her lush breasts and shapely derriere drew way too many ogling eyes. She caught Luis on a number of occasions licking his lips as he stared, oblivious to the fact that he had zero chance in hell with her.

"What did you think of my speech?" Luis whispered in her ear, causing a shudder of disgust to whip through her.

Maria tamped down on what she really wanted to say because several others were at the table watching them. Maria knew why she was there—she needed to keep her promise to her mom and sister. But she didn't have to play this game. She turned to him with a sly smile. "Do not speak to me. I'm here because you didn't give me a choice. We … are not friendly."

Turning away from Luis, the hairs on the back of Maria's neck stood up when she saw Futtaim's hot glare leveled on her. Maria wanted to sink into the floor as Futtaim gave Luis a curious nod.

From the conversation at the table, she learned that the turnout couldn't have been better. Politicians, business owners, and prominent community members were seated at every table. The sponsors of the gala, who Luis had been working with since he had been promoted, were sitting at his table. They were the ones who encouraged him to get on the board of the Wellbound, as it would be mutually beneficial.

Banquet staff, dressed in robes and dresses, cleared everything after the meal. Futtaim stood and walked around the table, cutting the space between him and Maria down to an uncomfortable minimum.

"Mr. Fry, care to introduce me to your … beautiful friend?" Futtaim asked, his pronounced Middle Eastern accent thick with the effort to sound engaging.

Luis stood abruptly, all signs of his arrogant demeanor gone in a matter of seconds. The beads of sweat collecting on his forehead betrayed his earlier bravado. Maria flickered a gaze between the two men and connected more of the behind the scenes details than they would have thought possible. Maybe somehow she could find a way to get out from under Luis Fry's thumb. One thing for certain, she wasn't giving Luis what he wanted until he delivered on his promise. First.

* * *

Having worked with Futtaim for several years, Luis understood fully that he was not to be crossed.

Mr. Futtaim was fundamental in planning this event, even though his interests and requirements were questionable. The international business mogul requesting access to ten incarcerated or rehabilitated women with very specific criteria, didn't sit well with many members of the board. However, Luis collected the information without as much as a blink. Black, Hispanic, and Asian. No familial ties with people who would look for them. No drug charges. They had to be between the ages of nineteen and twenty-nine, tall, curvy, and beautiful.

Luis didn't ask many questions regarding the man's reasons, but he had an idea because he'd attended the parties Futtaim hosted before he visited Alabama. Luis had been the happy recipient of the best sex performed by the most exotic women he'd ever seen, his reward for accomplishing the tasks that were asked of him. Pulling women out of the system wasn't going to be easy, but Futtaim told him not to worry, and to just find the women. He would do the rest.

Several people in Futtaim's circle had disappeared under mysterious circumstances, Luis feared that if he screwed up one thing, he'd be found dead, or never found again. He was determined to stay on the man's good side. Tonight that would depend on Maria Sanchez since Futtaim had taken a special interest in her. If Futtaim sensed that she wouldn't cooperate or could be a loose cannon, they'd both be done.

Luis had briefed Maria on the importance of this night, but was still concerned that she wouldn't follow through. He had upped the ante by promising to have her mother and sister released within a few months. Thanks to calling in a few favors, he could manage it. What he couldn't survive is disappointing a man so dangerously well-connected internationally.

"Good evening, Mr. Futtaim," Luis said, hoping no one else heard the tremor in his voice. "Thank you again for your donation in support of this organization. We're going to do great things in Birmingham."

Futtaim held his gaze on Maria as if he wasn't listening to Luis for anything other than what he demanded.

"This is Maria. She has been assisting me on some … special assignments."

Futtaim held out his hand and Maria stood, reluctantly giving him hers. He slowly brought her hand up to his lips and kissed the top, peering into her eyes but failing to notice her gaze as she shifted her focus to Luis. Panic set in, and Luis realized that she was going to be trouble.

"Maria, it is a pleasure to meet you. Luis has told me how helpful you have been to our operation. My business in Nadaum will thrive because of your assistance, and we couldn't be more thankful." Futtaim released Maria's hand and inclined his head.

"Yes sir," Maria said, a chill running up her spine as she stared deep into Futtaim's cold, soulless eyes.

"I do hope you enjoy this evening. Our entertainers are the best from our clubs throughout the Middle East. It will be like nothing you have ever seen." Futtaim smiled and beckoned for Luis to join him.

As Futtaim and Luis moved away, Maria settled down at the table, her back stiff and hands folded neatly in her lap. She bowed her head, praying that Meghan and Sally didn't see her tonight after saying she wouldn't come. She certainly wouldn't know how to explain her presence, especially at Luis's table.

# *Chapter 22*

Rory had taken the opportunity to scan the ballroom as dinner was served, observing the people at each table carefully. He'd crossed paths with many of the guests through his business dealings in Birmingham and with The Castle.

Daron Kincaid, Kaleb Valentine, and Shaz Bostwick were all well affiliated with a number of people of influence and financial means in the United States by way of their own endeavors or business clients. Their reach had recently become international, as Kaleb and several others expanded their connections to Durabia by purchasing real estate. A few of the properties were being used to transition women into a normal day to day life.

Kaleb strutted over to Rory in a plum and gold Dashiki pant set looking like he was born into the royal family.

"Mr. Tannous."

Rory stood to receive him with a brotherly hug. "Kaleb Valentine," he said, giving him a pat on the back before releasing him. "How's everything? I thought Daron was meeting me tonight. Is there a problem?"

"He's coming in on the Red Eye. But he *did* send you a gift. Is there somewhere more private we can move to for a few?" Kaleb asked.

Rory nodded, then excused himself from the table before showing him to the smoking lounge which wasn't open to the event until later in the evening. When the door closed behind them, Kaleb slid a hand in his pants pocket and extracted a gunmetal and crystal tie tack designed to record audio and filter out background noise. He placed it in Rory's hand. "We need to have ears to figure out what is going on with your woman."

*My woman?* Why did he like the sound of that?

"How kind is Daron? And just my style." Rory rolled the jewel between his fingers before pinning it to the underside of his charcoal gray bow tie.

"Speaking of your woman," Kaleb flashed a mischievous grin while whipping a black velvet box from his pocket. "These are for Meghan," he said, slowly opening the box for dramatic effect.

"She gets diamonds?" Rory questioned with a hint of jealousy while wondering how he would present such a thing to Meghan. "What do these do?"

"They're equipped with audio capabilities. Daron can activate them remotely should you two be separated."

*Let's hope that doesn't happen*

"Excellent Thanks, KV."

Rory slipped the box into his tuxedo jacket and followed Kaleb to a nearby bar area.

"How are things with the family?" Kaleb inquired pulling out a credit card and handing it to the bartender. "A tequila and cranberry, please."

"Mom is great," Rory said, smiling. "Tarah, has become a whiz at Uno."

"I'll have to get Skylar and the girls and make a trip down here, just so they can play. My girls love to play Uno."

Luis left the table closest to the podium, distracting Rory from Kaleb. Taking note of his less-than-confident strut to the stage, Rory reflected on the confirmation call from Luis; something in his voice sounded shaken. Upon hearing Mr. Futtaim's name, the hairs on the back of Rory's neck stood. Even Kaleb stiffened.

*Something is off.*

Rory had attended an event in Nadaum that was put on by Futtaim's people. Beautiful women of every ethnic background danced and writhed as entertainment, practically crawling all over the drunk visiting Americans. He had never felt more uncomfortable in a social setting. Rory couldn't claim a trip to a strip club, not even when he attended college at University of Alabama.

Women were not to be used strictly for pleasure. Point, blank, period. Even in his few relationships, he made sure that by the time they parted ways, the women walked away better for the experience just as he had. And not merely on a sexual level. Most of the relationships ended because of his extensive travel and the energy he put into his life's mission. He told them from the beginning, but most were under the misguided belief that they could change him. Not so.

He understood the number of women in the sex industry who were truly in it because they loved the work was slim in comparison to those working because they were forced or had no other viable options to support themselves, their families, or their habits.

"I'm going to take a seat," Kaleb declared, glancing past Rory at the commanding presence marching across the room with locs down past his waist. People parted, giving him a wide berth. "I'm watching. Shaz is here. Daron is on his way. Don't lose that tack. It's live streaming."

"Got it."

Kaleb turned on his heels and danced back to his table.

Rory's glance zipped from table to table, recognizing five men in the room who were in attendance at that party, two were prominent businessmen who ran the Lakeside Federal Banks in Alabama—Anthony Cahill and Samuel Roache, a tax lawyer who had millions to spend after his donations were returned by the University of Alabama when news broke of the sexual harassment accusations made by the female interns under their supervision. The fact that these men had been at a party in

Nadaum hosted by Futtaim meant that whatever Daron suspected was going on in Birmingham was probably worse than even he knew.

* * *

Rory pushed his plate away and put a gold napkin on top to signal he was finished with his meal. He cleared his throat to get Lisa's attention, but also snagged Sally's, who seemed particularly disturbed by the amount of attention Lisa had given Rory throughout the night.

Lisa nodded her response.

Rory turned to Meghan and was met with perfectly shaped, yet furrowed eyebrows. She had barely touched her meal while watching the activity in the room, her observation landing on the nonverbal communication between Rory and Lisa, but more of a pointed interest with the woman seated at Luis Fry's table.

"What's with all of the nodding, you two?" Meghan questioned.

"My apologies, Meghan, but I think it's time we discuss why I'm here." He gestured to the dance floor when the DJ switched from the more fast-paced popular music he'd been playing all evening, to a slower number that instantly changed the vibe in the ballroom. "Shall we?"

Sally stood to join them, but Lisa yanked her back down in the seat.

# Chapter 23

Meghan melted into Rory's arms the moment they bypassed the dance floor and went straight to the private balcony overlooking the grounds of the Rossman Bridge Resort. A beautifully ornate water fountain with colorful lights that seemed to flicker in time with the music from inside cast a romantic glow over the couple.

Sweet scents of jasmine, grapefruit, and baby powder wafted in the air around Rory as he inhaled slow and steady, enjoying Meghan's fragrance and calming his racing heartbeat. He had never allowed himself to be this close to a client, but a conflict of interest was the farthest thing from his mind.

His gaze snapped to the glass and saw a number of people watching, so he locked the door from the outside in order to prevent anyone from invading their conversation.

Rory spun Meghan out into a twirl and brought her close; so close that he could feel her breath on his neck.

* * *

They danced for a short while, and she enjoyed the muscular feel of him, the woody scent of him, and the quiet strength he exuded. She hadn't felt the embrace of a man since she broke up with Luis Fry. When he told her he was going to work for the District Attorney's office as the lead prosecutor, his upward mobility came with an ultimatum that she didn't take kindly.

Meghan had never loved Luis. He had no problem with publicly humiliating her, even criticizing her choice of apparel when she didn't wear what he purchased. He kept the company of unscrupulous white-collar clients who financed his lifestyle, and fidelity was as foreign to him as life on Mars. But great sex made up for a number of his flaws, or at least it did until he wanted her to give up the one thing that centered her and brought peace. With his move to the DA's office, Luis demanded she shut down her non-profit operation because it would be bad for his career. That one thing, more than any other, made her question why she was with him anyway.

Something she did learn about the great Luis Fry, is that he didn't do a lot of thinking for himself. Considering his brilliant legal mind, he must've received a large stipend to throw away his most precious value—integrity.

Meghan only trusted herself thanks to those experiences, but the brief moments she'd spent with Rory tonight were already starting to change her mindset. His voice calmed her; his touch sent shivers of heat coursing through her body—a feeling she never could satisfy for herself even with all of her special little toys. Well, if she had to be honest, one of them was not quite so little.

His presence scared her as much as it excited her, and now wasn't a good time to let her feelings take over reasonable thinking.

"Who are you, really?" she whispered.

Rory gazed down into her eyes seriously for several moments, then his expression darkened as he broke their connection and leaned on the rail to put a little distance between them. "I've lived in Birmingham for twenty years," he said, "But my childhood was a little more complicated. Khalil Germaine, founder of The Castle, rescued my family from my father. He had taken my mother and forced her to stay in a marriage that turned abusive in Nadaum, after their honeymoon in Durabia."

Meghan's heart sank, but she remained silent because this was no light fare. She looked away for a moment, absorbing that piece of information that explained a lot of what she had found out about him.

"I was recently named the Knight of Birmingham after my shelter opened outside of Durabia. Reno, along with some of his King brothers, have shelters across the world with the same vision as mine." His darkened blue eyes searched hers for a moment before adding, "I'm back in Birmingham for a few months to make sure my businesses and home are in order before I return my full attention to what has made me the proudest. Helping women escape marriages where they are enslaved and under the Sharia law, in the way that Khalil helped my mother."

A knock on the glass door of the balcony startled them both, and Meghan missed Rory's warmth.

He turned to the door to open it, keeping Meghan positioned behind him as if he was her protective shield.

"Can I help you," Rory asked as a tall, wiry hostess on the other side of the door.

"Good evening, sir. I was asked by one of the sponsors to see why the balcony was locked. We need to keep this space open for safety reasons."

Rory nodded. "My apologies ma'am. We needed to have a private conversation. We'll be in shortly."

The woman gave them a lingering look filled with suspicion, but said nothing more as she swept away back towards the glittering crowd.

"I know the basics from what Lisa told Reno," Rory said, putting his focus back on Meghan. "They're missing. No one's helping. I get that. Give me the most startling part of the equation so I can start there."

Meghan lowered her gaze to the ground and when she looked up at him she said, "Their social security numbers don't come up in anyone's system anymore. It's like they never existed."

"Means someone with a lot of power is pulling the strings," Rory mused. "And we're not talking about the State level, this sounds like someone higher up."

"Exactly," she conceded. "The sheriff and the D.A. have done zilch. Even though they have proof."

"What do the women have in common?"

"They all fit a certain profile," she replied and gave him the criteria ending with, "No family ties aside from kids in foster care. Some of them were looking forward to reuniting with their families upon their release. Most of them only had a month or two left in their sentences. They were non-violent offenders. Besides their ethnic background and age, they all had similar body types." She inhaled sharply, trying not to break down in front of him. The fear that her friend had met with a horrible end was more likely with each passing day. "Except one." Meghan's voice trembled as she tried to hold her composure. "My friend, Candace. She doesn't fit the profile other than her ethnicity. She has family and kids who live with her mother and aunts. She has people who love her." The tears Meghan fought so hard to stop, escaped down her cheeks. "I love her."

Rory pulled her hands apart and brought her into his arms. She stayed there for what seemed like forever as he allowed her the moment needed to unburden her soul to a man who was actually going to help. Not tell her she was crazy. Not tell her that the women were nothing. Not tell her that she was off base because nothing like this could happen on American soil. She knew that he believed her.

"Before we head back in, I need to give you something." Rory pulled the black velvet box Kaleb gave him out of his pocket.

"Oh no sir, this isn't happening," Meghan said, causing Rory to laugh. "After all that trust stuff, I had to…"

He opened the box to show Meghan.

"As much as I'd love to give you a gift of such stunning beauty, these are from Kings of The Castle. They are designed to live stream audio while you're wearing them. Some intel they've received informed them that some of the people attending this event could be key to in this case, so we need to be monitored. They need to know what's happening and respond accordingly."

Meghan appeared unsure. "Listen," Rory said, motioning to his tie tack. "I have one too. This is a safety measure that is necessary after what you've already been through this week."

Meghan hesitated, then took out her pearl teardrop earrings.

"If you don't mind, may I help put these in Madam?" Rory asked with a grin.

Meghan couldn't deny that she quite enjoyed the idea of such an intimate exchange with this man. "Yes," she said, the huskiness in her voice returning, which caught her off guard.

# Chapter 24

Rory processed all that Meghan had shared as they moved back to the dance floor and made a few moves on the next song that blared throughout the venue.

"Meghan, you mentioned your team," he said dipping her low, causing a smile to spread on her lips. "I've only met Sally. Who else works for you?"

Meghan's eyes widened at his question as he led her to the anteroom that housed the silent auction items, away from the music and the crowds. "Maria Sanchez. I hired her and Sally at the same time. While Sally had been incarcerated, Maria was a little different."

"In what way?"

"Her father brutally raped her, and her mother and sister killed him when they walked in on him in the act. They both received lengthy sentences, despite all the evidence of what the man had done. Maria has been working with me to help free them while also serving clients."

Rory inhaled, absorbing that unexpected tidbit of info before his gaze flickered to Shaz, who wound his way through the throng of guests and was aiming for the men's room.

"But she's been acting distant lately," Meghan whispered in an absent tone, but it caused Rory to refocus on what she said. "She hasn't been returning calls, she's been late and flustered at the office several times, and she hadn't been participating in meetings until we cornered her the day Luis Fry was there. She told us she wasn't interested in this event, but then she's here, hiding out at his table."

Rory scanned the ballroom through the doors of the auction room, all while he was conversing with Meghan. The banquet was bustling with potential donors who were now in the networking and fundraising stage of things. A few more familiar faces had materialized as he listened to Meghan talk about Maria. He spotted Luis crossing the dance floor with a young woman in a gold dress that looked as though it had been painted on. Though smiling, they seemed to be in some type of heated conversation.

Luis redirected his focus and gripped the woman's arm. Soon they were walking toward Rory and Meghan, while the woman stayed two paces behind.

Rory released Meghan from his hold, immediately missing the physical connection, and turned to greet Luis.

Meghan glared as she turned. "Maria, what are you doing here? With him?"

Rory swept a gaze across all of the parties but zeroed in on Maria's instant and obvious discomfort.

"Ahh, Rory, I see you've been acquainted with Birmingham's infamous hero, Meghan Turner," Luis announced, his condescending tenor grating on Rory's nerves.

Luis extended a hand to Meghan, which she refused.

"Okay then." Luis chuckled and lowered his hand back to his side. "Still a little bitter about things, I see."

"Not bitter, just cautious," Meghan snapped. "Don't know where your hands have been since they seemed to travel from bed to bed along with the rest of you."

*Well damn.*

"I don't have to pretend to be cordial in a social setting," she explained. "I leave that for people who have to actually kiss your ass to get things done."

*Double damn. Meghan—two. Luis, a negative zero.*

A vein throbbed at Luis' temple, but he had the presence of mind not to attempt a comeback. "It's good to see you, man," Luis said. "Let me introduce you to my date tonight, the lovely—"

"Maria Sanchez," Rory said, finishing the sentence. "Wonderful to meet you. We were just talking about you."

Luis laughed as Maria grew pale while still trying to avoid eye contact with Meghan.

*Definitely the place to start looking.*

"Well, great then. Maria, this is my good friend Rory," he continued despite Maria's fidgeting and visible discomfort. "We go way back. I personally invited him to attend in hopes of a large donation from The Castle to support The Wellbound House. Rory, did you decide if you're attending the party later?" He put his arm around Maria's waist and practically yanked her to his side. "We'll both be there. I'd tell you to bring Meghan, but I don't think it'd be her scene."

"I think I'm good," Rory replied, winking at Meghan as he made an instant decision to send one of the Kings in his stead. "I'm in great company, and I'd like it to stay that way."

Meghan's head whipped to Rory, and she frowned.

"All right, come find me later," Luis said, but he was none too happy at the answer. "We definitely have things to talk about."

Rory narrowed his gaze on Luis but did not respond to his invitation.

"Meghan, shall we?" Rory placed a hand on Meghan's back, guiding her away from the tense couple. He knew meeting up with that man at any time would be dangerous but felt confident he was ready for anything Luis Fry might try to do.

Meghan pulled away from Rory's touch and stepped out of their intimate space.

"I can't believe it," she seethed barely above a whisper, throwing her hands up. "I knew you were too good to be true. I let my guard down. This gorgeous man here to save the day and all the pretty little women.

You're just like *them*. Friends with Luis Fry is all I need to know. I can't believe I told you everything. You're probably behind all of this."

Rory grasped Meghan's arm, and turned her to face him full on. Her eyes filled with fire, rage, and sadness, something he'd do anything to change. He never wanted to be the cause of it again.

"Meghan, please, breathe," Rory implored. "I am not friends with Luis. We went to the same college. I am here to help. I asked you to trust me and at the first sign of trouble, you're ready to abort the mission. Without even giving me the opportunity to explain."

Meghan narrowed her gaze on Rory, jerked out of his grasp, and stormed away.

Rory had his work cut out for him. Finding out what Luis was up to and trying to keep Meghan safe. All while she had a huge block of mistrust in her heart, which was the first obstacle he needed to overcome.

# Chapter 25

"Meghan, wait," Rory said, running after her. He was trying to calm Meghan down, but his demands fell upon deaf ears as she continued to walk ahead of him aiming for the Ladies' room. "Wait, I'll follow you wherever you run off to." Rory crossed the distance, struggling to catch up to Meghan who moved across the ballroom as if she were wearing skates and not heels. She was a lot steadier on her feet when she was pissed off, than she was on the way into the building a few hours ago.

Meghan spun around, stopping Rory in his tracks. "I do not need an escort," she shouted, drawing looks from other guests as she marched past him.

"Listen, I know you're angry, though I'm not sure I understand why yet," Rory explained, slowing down his chase. "After all you've shared tonight, and then Maria showing up with Luis, and his strange reaction when he saw me with you, I just don't feel comfortable with you being alone until we understand exactly what we're dealing with."

The two were almost to the restrooms when Meghan glanced over her shoulder, her face red hot with anger.

"Fine. Stay out here," she said with a dismissive wave. "Whatever. Do not come in."

Rory nodded, accepting Meghan's demand. Leaning against the wall next to a set of doors directly across from the women's restroom, he crossed his arms and waited for her to reemerge, hopefully in a better mood. Those kidneys work a little different after emptying three glasses of wine.

With Meghan out of his sight, Rory took the opportunity to process all that he'd just learned. Maria, who had been distant at work, showed up as Luis Fry's date. Whatever Meghan and Luis's history was, it appeared to have been a disaster then and volatile now. The party that was taking place later sounded like it would rival the ones in Nadaum. The sponsor of the gala, Futtaim, was a known link to human trafficking in the Middle East. Feeding all of this information to the Kings would give them the concrete proof and a lead to locate Candace and the rest of the women who'd been taken.

Murmuring voices came through an open door beside him, one of them sounded familiar.

"The five women will be pulled tonight," Maria revealed.

"Very good," Futtaim said.

"You will be happy with this group, sir," a slightly familiar voice crowed and sounded as if it were being played on a speakerphone. "Maria showed us pictures, and this is the best group yet. Tall, huge breasts, and nice, light skin. Even a spunky little Asian. This is exactly what your clients requested. Fry is getting their records wiped, and the van will be at Tutwiler at midnight sharp. Make sure your guards are ready."

Rory held his breath, hoping he was wrong and scooted a little closer to the doorway to better hear the account. His neck muscles became tight, and his temples ached listening to the information the next voice brought.

*That sounds like Malakai.*

Meghan reappeared and two women, who were holding an animated conversation veered away from her. Her eagle-eyed gaze locked in on his. She tilted her head, and he placed a finger to his lips and beckoned her forward.

She blinked twice as though clearing out her memory, then she speed-walked toward him. He gestured for her to stay beside him, pointing a finger to his ear.

"Everything is a go, lady and gentlemen," Luis said with a clap, happiness coloring his tone. "They no longer exist. Well done, Maria. Your sister and mother will remain safe for another month. We'll only need twenty more women to fulfill our commitment to Mr. Futtaim. Then your family will be released."

Meghan's eyes went wide, and Rory gave her a warning glare to remain silent.

"What are you talking about, Luis?" Maria spoke with hatred in her tone. "You already have five. This makes ten. That's all I agreed to."

"Is this what you told her?" Futtaim questioned, and there was a gruffness in his tone that signaled his displeasure.

"Spanish is her first language, sir," Luis explained, with a nervous shiver in his voice marked either by fear or reverence. Rory guessed a cocktail of both. "She may have misunderstood me."

"Fuck you, Luis," Maria declared, before the sound of something clamoring against the wall. "I have a great command of the King's English, and I know how to count. This is nothing like the agreement we talked about."

A sharp sound, like a slap, echoed and caused Meghan to flinch.

"I do not know who you think you are, little woman," Futtaim warned. "But if you don't want to see your sister disappear like these women, you'd better watch how you speak to this man."

A whimper and gasp followed that assertion.

"Women do not have a place raising their voice to any man, especially one who holds the key to the freedom of your loved ones," Futtaim chastised. "Learn respect, woman."

Another strike and Rory moved forward.

Meghan's hand snaked out to hold him in place as Maria sobbed. Footsteps forced them to action as Rory guided Meghan away from the door and slid out his phone, pretending to be in the midst of a conversation as Futtaim walked out with Luis right behind him.

Over Meghan's shoulder, Rory saw Maria run out of the doors, across the hall, and into the restroom.

"Meghan, be an ear, *only* that," he warned, gesturing for her to go back into the restroom. "Be an ear. Do not give away what we know. That is our only advantage to finding Candace. If she tells them you know something, they'll go so far underground we'll never find her or any of the others. Right now they're working from a position of arrogance and privilege. The Kings will need them to stay that way. That's when folks get sloppy. Looks like I'll need to go to that party to get a line on things."

Meghan's chest heaved in an effort to take in a solid breath.

"Do you trust me now?" he whispered.

She nodded vigorously, and only then did she release her breath. They now knew the who, but then again, they'd kind of narrowed that down early on. The *how* of things is what was going to take some unravelling.

"Go," he said, nodding towards the restroom. She took off, flying past the room but paused when a woman nearly barreled into her.

*We have a problem and need to mobilize quickly. Kaleb is here. How soon are you going to be here?* Rory texted Daron before sliding his phone into a pocket just in time.

"Rory, man," Luis bellowed with more cheer than Rory wanted to stomach. "Come here. Meet our sponsor."

Rory flickered a gaze towards the restroom entrance, hoping that Meghan was playing it cool. The only way to earn and keep her trust was to let her play a part. Everyone working together for the common good. Since it looked like the other side had been working in the opposite direction.

"This is Anwar Futtaim, President of the Futtaim Foundation, who is footing the bill for this gala. This is—"

"I know who he is," Rory said, trying to keep his voice level.

Futtaim nodded to Rory as Luis Fry's narrowed gaze bounced between Futtaim and Rory.

"Did you decide on joining us tonight? It would be great to introduce you to some people. It's been too long, bro."

"I think I will attend for a little bit," Rory replied, giving him a smile and avoiding the hand that Luis tried to clamp on his shoulder. "Text me the details, and I'll see you there."

Rory didn't want to go, but he felt he needed to, so that he could understand more about the underground criminal element that was operating in Birmingham. He needed to learn who else was involved stateside, and how far outside of the country the deals were going. He was glad he now had that unforeseen advantage since Futtaim and Luis had no idea he overheard their conversation.

# Chapter 26

Meghan stood in the bride's room area of the restroom, reserved for wedding parties. Her thoughts of pretending to fix her make-up were dashed when she realized her purse was still at the dinner table. She blotted a tissue on her forehead and waited for Maria to emerge.

Questions swirled in Meghan's mind as she went over the details of her tumultuous relationship with her former lover, but then thoughts of Rory took over. She was on the fence about how to feel about the man whose touch brought a welcome heat to places she'd long thought had iced over. But her brain kept reminding her, she knew very little about him. If he was connected to a crook like Luis Fry how was she supposed to trust him?

Bringing her in to hear, firsthand, what Luis was up to. That was the best move he could have made. If Rory was involved, hearing that would have blown up his spot as well.

As Meghan had no more reasons to remain in the restroom, she washed her hands yet another time. Maria came out of the stall, a sob escaping her mouth as she glanced at Meghan before she bent over and released dinner into the sink.

*Really? There was a whole toilet back there and you want to put dinner in the sink?*

Pausing to collect her thoughts, Meghan calculated her next move. She could walk out and never look back, or she could help her friend and try to figure out what was going on. The latter was best because Rory was counting on her.

"Maria," Meghan whispered as she walked up behind her, grabbing some paper towels and handing them over. Helping her to stand, Meghan took another paper towel and wiped her cheek while turning on the water to rinse everything down the drain. "Maria—"

Meghan waited, quietly taking in the red hand imprinted across Maria's cheek and decided a less threatening tactic was best. "Forgot the girl code, eh?"

Maria covered the spot on her face, her hand not nearly as big as the print that remained. "Meghan, I'm so sorry. I'm so sorry," Maria cried, talking so fast her normally absent Spanish accent appeared. "They threatened to take mi madre y mi hermana if I didn't help."

She looked up at Meghan, those dark brown eyes imploring her friend and boss to understand. "Luis said they would disappear, and I'd never know if they were dead or alive if I didn't help him. He said I couldn't talk to you about it, or he'd take them. But if I helped, he'd help keep them safe and get them out if we accomplished the mission." She bent over again, and Meghan inched back out of the direct line of fire, just in case.

"And I thought we did," Maria said after a moment. "I didn't know what they were doing. I didn't know about Candace until you said something. I heard you say she was missing, and that's why I haven't been back. This is all my fault. I'm so sorry."

Meghan's heart sank as she processed everything Maria admitted. The betrayal was even deeper than walking in on Luis with a woman on all fours and him pumping away as if the woman had done him wrong.

"Sweetheart, please, breathe. Slow down," she pleaded, leading Maria to a nearby chaise. "Come, let's sit. It'll be okay. I can help you now."

"No, Meghan, you don't understand. That man, Futtaim, he hit me." Maria tried to pull away from Meghan's hold, but she wouldn't let her. "If they know you know, they'll kill us both. I have to go. I've said too much."

Meghan pulled Maria's head against her shoulder.

Sally and Lisa walked in, and those pantsuits had lost every ounce of polish since they were now plastered on their bodies. The D J had switched to House music and those two hadn't left the dance floor until now.

Meghan gestured them over, and turned back to Maria. "Tell me everything, and together we'll find a way to get you out of this." She paused, giving Maria the opportunity to decide.

"I've been copying files from JB," Maria explained, sniffling, her head bowed as she wiped a hand over her face. "First it was just cases that Luis specifically requested, because he'd seen the women in court. Then we ran out of those women, so I went into the backlog of clients waiting for assignment."

Meghan and Sally glanced at each other before Meghan stood and paced the floor, rubbing her stomach. She knew she spent too much time outside of the office rallying for funds for the program and searching out volunteers. And all this was going on right under her nose.

"I provided Luis with at least one hundred and fifty potential women," Maria admitted then stopped and watched Meghan, a fresh wave of tears rolling down her face. "He told me only ten were needed from me, and I'd be done, but he lied. He has the five you know about, and there are five more being taken tonight."

Sally and Lisa blew a collective sigh as Meghan halted her pacing, reclaiming the seat next to Maria.

"He told me there would be a test," Maria confessed. "I thought it would be if you started questioning me, but now I realize it must have been Candace. To see if I cracked when someone close to JB disappeared." Maria brought her hand to her cheek, the injured area growing darker. "I'm in too deep. I'm scared. Futtaim is an evil man. I felt it when Luis introduced us at the dinner table. Like the ancestors were sending me a warning. But they sent it much too late." She locked gazes with Meghan. "I owe my mother and sister everything, but I can't give anything if I lose my life."

All that could be heard was the bass beats of music playing outside of the doors while all three women shook their heads.

"Well damn. What a mess this is, young lady," Sally said breaking the quiet. Her thin gray eyebrows met in the middle of her forehead. "I'm so angry that you have compromised our work and the women we're trying to help. I understand that you were trying to free your sister and mother, but that was just plain selfish."

Meghan nodded. "I wish you would have trusted us enough to say something sooner. We would have tried to help you."

"What do we do now?" Maria asked.

"We have someone—" Meghan shook her head, and Lisa quickly nudged Sally into silence.

"We will figure something out," Meghan said, taking in Sally's frown, but Lisa's glare guaranteed they would have a discussion later.

Sally smoothed a hand over Maria's bare shoulder, a pitiful glare was all she could muster as compassion. "Honestly, I don't want to help someone who put us all in such grave danger, but for you and this organization, I will."

"Thank you," Maria sobbed. "I'm so sorry again. My sister and mother gave up their lives to save me from my father. I swore I'd spend the rest of mine protecting them until we can be together again. I didn't know what to do. But we will work together now."

Meghan released Maria from her embrace and leveled a worried gaze on her. "You can't be seen with us. It'll cause too much suspicion and put you in danger," she warned. "Please do what you came here to do, and text me when you're home safe. And for God's sake, respond to your text messages or answer your damn phone from now on. We're in this together now. Be careful, and don't make mention to anyone that you have been in contact with us."

"Yes, Ma'am," Maria replied through sniffles.

"Now … let's get you put together now, so you can get back out there."

Sally crossed her arms in front of her slight chest and bounced her knee while she waited for Meghan to finish helping Maria touch up her make-up.

Maria brushed her long brown hair out, straightened her dress, looked in the mirror one final time before nodding to her co-workers and leaving the restroom.

"What in the hell are we going to do with that one?" Sally's southern drawl was out in full force. "She put our whole organization and all of our women at risk. She had access to private information on these women that not even the court system had. They trusted us and now every file she has touched means another woman in danger. How can we even begin to fix this? Bless her ever-loving dumbass heart."

Meghan laughed to keep from crying. She didn't know how to answer the question, but she knew she had to do something.

"And why did you keep me from mentioning Rory," Sally asked.

"It's best that we know everything she knows, but that she doesn't know everything we know."

Lisa gave an appreciative nod.

Meghan shifted her focus to Lisa. "I need you to go out there and let Rory know that we should reconvene at the bar that's on the lower level so we can figure out what's what."

* * *

An answering message pinged on his cell at the same time a visibly shaken Meghan stepped out of the restroom, into the bar several minutes behind Lisa and Sally.

"Greetings, ladies," Rory said, flashing a smile at Meghan as if she was the only person in the room.

"Hey Rory. Has Lisa filled you in?" Meghan inquired, impressed that he wasn't angry considering her earlier tantrum.

"Yes, she did." Rory leaned into Meghan's ear and whispered. "I'm glad to see you're feeling better. I'm sorry that you misunderstood the relationship."

"Listen, you don't have anything to apologize for," Meghan said. "You said I have to trust you. I have to learn how to do that. None of us know what is going on. Women we care about are in danger, and you were sent to help us. That's all we have to go on for now. So, where do we start?"

Rory gave Meghan another smile, keeping his thoughts of how wonderful she was to himself. He hoped that there was more to learn about her beyond her tough exterior. "Can I get you something to drink?"

"Jameson and coke, please," Meghan replied, returning Rory's attention with a foxy smile.

"Two Jameson and cokes, please," Rory requested of the bartender, reaching in his blazer pocket and extracting a credit card and cash. Dropping a crisp, folded twenty-dollar bill into the brandy-snifter shaped tip jar, Rory turned to Meghan and said, "Where we start is you telling me what I need to know about Luis Fry. I need some ammunition going into that party tonight. If they're taking those five new women offshore, we need to act before that happens."

Chapter 27

The cell in Rory's pocket vibrated with a notification. Luis had sent the address and time for the afterparty. The gala still had an hour before it ended, but the festivities for the other event were about to start.

*I'll be a bit late to the party, Luis.* He texted back.

"What do you want to know?" Meghan asked, receiving the glass of dark Amber fluid from Rory's hand. "I thought you said you went to college with him."

"I did, but can a couple of freshman classes give you a real idea of a person's character?"

"I don't suppose so." Meghan took a sip from her glass, then placed it on the table. She scanned the room, measuring the words she wanted to speak about the one relationship that made being single a desired option. "First of all, don't judge me."

"Not a problem."

"In short, we worked together in the district attorney's office and dated for three years until I established The Journey Beyond program. He broke up with me. He said it was bad for business."

Rory's eyebrows shot up as he ran a hand through his hair. "Wow."

She shrugged. "That's what I said. Well, I cried, mostly because the sex was amazing. So much so, that I still miss it even a year later."

Rory chuckled, and her eyes snapped to him.

"What's so funny?" Meghan demanded.

"Most women don't make a habit of openly talking about past lovers with me."

"I'm not most women," she countered. "And we aren't lovers so …"

"There is that," he shot back. "Anything else?"

"He's an investor of sorts … in the program."

"Investor?"

"He shares the title of one of the transition houses. We have a five-year payment agreement for me to buy him out. The other two houses are from community donors."

Rory tossed back the rest of his drink and wiped a hand over his face, and slid the empty glass toward the bartender.

"What's wrong?" Meghan asked, raising her eyebrows.

"That community donor is Anwar Futtaim," he said. "He's a prominent businessman in Nadaum, a neighboring city to Durabia. It seems that American women of color are his newest venture.

"He's running a tight operation in the Middle East, targeting sales to prominent white businessmen who travel there for extended work contracts. He owns oil fields in the Middle East, a chain of restaurants, several resorts worldwide, and is invested in black market military firearms. However, sometimes American travelers want more … intimate activities while away from home, I guess. He tried to stop me from opening my shelter because his brother's American wife was one of my first clients."

"This is crazy," Meghan exclaimed.

Rory searched the area, meeting Sally's gaze, despite the fact that she was in a separate, private conversation with Lisa.

"Five more women will be picked up at Tutwiler prison at midnight," he said, showing her his phone and the information that Daron Kincaid had managed to find out, that also confirmed what they had heard. "He's been using a woman at Willingham's office and a woman at the governor's office to wipe their records. My King brothers are setting some things in motion as we speak. I have to go to the event to lay eyes on the customers."

Meghan's eyes grew wide, her heart pumped against her chest as she took that in.

"I know this is unprecedented, and we've only just met, but with everything going on right now—Bradland, Maria, Luis, Futtaim; I need you to stay at my home tonight. And maybe as long as we're working to shut this operation down. It's safe and secluded, and no one will suspect you're there."

Meghan choked and almost spit out her drink. "No. Way. In. Hell," she declared, her blue eyes as wide as saucers.

Rory shot a glance over his shoulder, then met Meghan's gaze intently as he whispered into her ear. "I have a large home with a staff and several extra rooms. My mother, brother, and sister also live on my estate. Whatever is going on, you're not safe in your home. They know where you live. And as much as we would like to trust Maria, we can't, not until she knows her mother and sister will be safe."

He placed a hand on her shoulder. "So, I'm sorry, but I'm not taking no for an answer. I'll drive you to your apartment to collect some things for a few days, and you'll stay with me."

Rory imagined what was going through her mind while she stood before him looking worried and defeated, her blue eyes growing dark and glassy. He thought he understood her angst—a stranger inviting her to his home to keep her safe from formidable forces was unheard of. He wished he were extending the invitation under more pleasant circumstances. In the little time he'd spent with Meghan, he found himself drawn to her. Her determination. Her beauty. Her compassion for humankind.

Meghan feverishly tapped her cell phone screen while Rory checked the time on his Tag Heuer watch.

"I wasn't raised to be that type of girl, but I guess I'm going home with you tonight," Meghan sighed, giving him a sideways grin.

Rory smiled, relishing the twinkle of what could only be mischief in Meghan's eyes.

* * *

Meghan rubbed her temples, feeling the tinge of a monster headache coming on. In all of her days as an advocate, she'd never seen a day like the one she was having.

She woke up marked as a moving target of the Bradland Boys, fell at the feet of the man who was supposed to help her rescue missing women, and now had an invitation to his estate because he believed she might be more of a target now that she knows more of the truth. However, the last part—staying in a protected zone—might not be a bad thing.

# Chapter 28

"Daron thinks he's located the first five women who went missing," Rory explained, just above a whisper.

Reading the message from Daron on his phone. The last vestiges of conversations and footsteps from the remaining guests milling around made him more aware of his surroundings. "Sally, Lisa, I need to get Meghan home. I'll make sure to keep you abreast of any changes."

"Good night, you two," Lisa chirped with a wink. "Try to have a little fun and do *everything* we would do."

Meghan rolled her eyes, held in the smile and the laugh she wanted to let loose. "Really, Lisa? He's here on business. I don't know about him, but I have no time for a relationship or even random what I could hope to be mind-blowing sex, for that matter. I have to find Candace and the others and still run the program." She tapped a finger on Lisa's chest. "That's where my mind is, and you should get *yours* out of the gutter."

"No need to debate," Rory teased. "Just business tonight. We have women to save. Lisa, would you and Sally mind bringing Meghan's car to my place? I'll text you the address. Ask for James at the gate. He'll take it from there, and you can go home with Sally,"

"Anything for the Knight in shining…eh sexy formal wear," Lisa teased.

Meghan rifled through her purse and tossed the keys over.

"You two be safe and have a good night," Rory said, taking Meghan by the hand again, escorting her to his car and settling her inside.

"Where to, Madam?" Rory asked, pulling on his seat belt. Flashing a grin, he placed his hands on the steering wheel,

"Siri, play … Nothing Else Matters by Metallica."

"Homewood," Meghan replied, her dry tone hinting at defeat. She stared out of the window at the passing buildings, greenery, and city lights as she chastised herself for letting Rory get too close so soon. As she became intoxicated with the scent of Bulgari Man in Black, Meghan wondered if it was Rory or the whiskey that made her feel as if she was on cloud nine. Had to be the whiskey. A Jameson Rarest vintage could do that. Definitely the whiskey.

*Do you trust me …*

Rory shook his head as his smile diminished. "Has anyone ever told you that your strength is sexy?"

Meghan gazed at Rory, her full red lips parting, but not relinquishing a single sound. Instead, her fingers laced then unlaced on her lap.

"I mean, in a world where a lot of women are waiting for a superhero, you're out here wearing the cape and saving the world." He nodded, and she felt his words were sincere. "It's pretty impressive work you're doing."

"I just want a good life, hell, a phenomenal life for all women," she said, leaning back on the leather headrest. "But especially for women who are most disenfranchised. How is it fair that women who are supporting or protecting their families get penalized at two to three times the rate of white women? Going to prison for years for killing the men that beat them within their last breaths? Or for stealing a box of crackers to feed their children? A woman who looks like me can bat an eyelash and say kiss my ass and get away with murder." She angled so her focus was totally on him. "What I do doesn't make me strong. It's more than the right thing to do."

Rory had many friends who were women, but in his history only one relationship had transformed into a true commitment. *Emotionally unavailable*. Those words echoed in his memory, the painful description the last woman he loved used for him before walking out the doors of the estate.

Getting past the images of his father beating his mother was a struggle, and remembering it each time he received a new wife at his shelter caused him to be closed off, even when he wanted to love more deeply.

However, Meghan's strength and compassion added to everything wonderful about her, and he wanted to know her better. Rory thought Meghan could be a good friend to have, but for the first time in a long time he also considered trying his hand at love. She would understand him more than any others.

"Is it too soon to ask to have the pleasure of holding your hand?" He kept his eyes on the road as he made this soft and tender request.

Meghan smiled as she laced her fingers through his, a touch that sent electricity through his body, energizing him, giving him life at that very moment.

Rory drove through the city holding Meghan's hand to keep her from fidgeting, caressing her thumb with his as the music played. Both swayed to the sound of the electric guitars, but said nothing. Even though it wasn't an uncomfortable silence, Rory felt there was tension in the air.

"I know Birmingham has its flaws," Rory said, breaking the silence. "but I've always loved the skyline on a clear night. Something about the lights and a quiet city just brings me peace."

Meghan's gaze raked over him—thick raven hair, well-formed shoulders, slight muscular build, ruggedly handsome, and sea-blue eyes. She smiled, seeing the vein pulsing at the base of his neck. She dared not look any further down to save them both any possible embarrassment.

*Trusting him may be easier than I thought.*

"I agree," Meghan conceded, allowing the conversation to sweep aside concerns for Candace, at least for the moment. "City lights are beautiful."

Rory cleared his throat, and Meghan's smile broke wide.

"When I take you to my home, I'll show you to the guest suite in my quarters. I hope you don't mind me leaving you to relax for the evening.

I need to see what's happening at Futtaim's. I have to see how he and Luis are making these exchanges happen."

"I don't mind," Meghan replied. "You said your King brothers are on top of things. You asked me to trust you, and you trust them. I'm not at all interested in being anywhere Luis is right now."

"Maria will be there." He gave her a sideways glance before putting his eyes on the road. "I may need to make sure she's safe. Besides, if I don't turn up it will raise suspicions, and we can't have that. I have a history with Futtaim, and if something goes wrong at this point, I'm afraid it could also bring danger to my operation. He suspects that I'm part of an underground network that directly helps women to escape his clutches, and others like him."

She was silent for a moment, then said, "No problem. I do need to relax after the day I've had. But I can't stay hidden away all weekend. I'd like to be able to see my family in the morning to let them know I'm all right. They've invited me for brunch."

Rory gave Meghan a questioning glance and narrowed his gaze. "It's not safe for you to drive alone right now."

"You can inspect my car before I leave in the morning," Meghan suggested as she withdrew her hand back to her lap. "No one knows I'll be at your estate."

Rory flickered a gaze at Meghan, trying to find the words to argue his point, but he simply repeated, "It's not safe for you to drive alone right now."

"It'll be fine. I can't lose my freedom," Meghan pleaded with Rory until they arrived at her apartment. "I've already agreed to stay at your place tonight."

Rory parked the car and went to open her door. Not responding to her assertions he said, "I'm coming in with you."

Heat flashed to Meghan's cheeks and ears. "Rory, my apartment is not prepared for guests. It's a mess because I was rushing to get ready for tonight. I can't let you in, I'm sorry."

Rory chuckled, shaking his head. "Fine. I'll wait outside, independent woman."

Meghan released a small puff of air as she opened the door just enough to squeeze in so he couldn't see, then closed and locked the door behind her. A handwritten note on the kitchen counter in Sue Ellyn's scratchy handwriting caught her attention. *A citation?*

She inhaled, deciding to deal with it when all of this blew over. She would be seriously pissed if Luis' antics made her lose her apartment; she certainly couldn't afford anything this nice in another area of Homewood.

Meghan dashed into the bathroom, stripped, washed quickly, and donned new undies and changed into her favorite black sweat suit and comfy black Brooks Levitate shoes to wear. There was no need to be sexy—he wouldn't even be there. She washed her face, pulled hair up into a high ponytail, threw a few days' worth of clothes into her duffle bag, two running kits, and her Xero running shoes. She added a toiletry bag, phone chargers, tidied up the joint, then turned out all the lights, grabbed her keys, and headed to her door. She paused for a minute when she heard voices outside.

*Good Lord. Not Sue Ellyn.*

She swung the door open to save Rory from whatever that old woman had to say, but it was too late.

"Ohhh, there you are," Sue Ellyn crooned. "How dare you leave this handsome young man waiting on your doorstep. He's the kind you want in your bed, not waiting outside your door, young lady."

Meghan's jaw went slack. Sue Ellyn had no filter, but Meghan thought she'd exercise restraint with complete strangers who were visiting residents of the building. Clearly, Sue Ellyn was in rare form as she stood at her front door dressed in a hot pink floral housecoat with one hand on her hip.

Rory faked a cough and cleared his throat, obviously, holding back his laughter.

"Maybe if you had him around more often, you wouldn't have had the trouble you've had this week," Sue Ellyn continued. "I was telling your friend about all the drama you've caused. Did you get the note I left on your counter? Your apartment is a mess; you should be ashamed."

"Yes Ma'am," she said, unwilling to protest by saying she had cleaned up. "But you're not supposed to enter my apartment without permission."

"Well, missy, your fire detector was going off, and after all that's going on around here, who knows what happened."

Meghan wasn't sure if she believed that but didn't have the time to care.

"It just went off?" Rory asked, his gaze narrowing on the woman. He brushed past Meghan and into the house.

"Rory, this is a gross invasion of privacy. You can't just come in here—"

His glare shut her down.

He ruffled through the utility drawer and pulled out a screwdriver, then grabbed a chair from her café table and climbed up. He peered up at the smoke alarm before taking it apart. He was so focused on that little piece of equipment that Meghan didn't want to break his concentration.

Rory pulled out a tiny black dot and held it on the tip of his finger so Meghan could see it.

"What's that?"

"Someone wants to make sure they know everything you're up to," he answered. "If we check the office, I'm betting some are placed there as well."

"They bugged me?" Meghan said, her heart rate increasing at the thought. "Who would do such a thing."

"You know exactly who did it," Rory said, jumping down and replacing the chair. "So no more pushback when I put things in place to keep you safe."

"But—"

"Meghan."

"Fine," she snapped.

Sue Ellyn tipped in. "I was just telling Mr. Tayak that—"

"It's Tannous, Ma'am," Rory corrected. "You can call me Rory."

"Rory. I was just telling *Rory* that I left you a note saying if one more thing happened, you would be out of here," she grumbled, wagging a bony finger at Meghan. "I can't have this type of activity in my building. I hope you get your shit together, young lady. Good night. And don't leave this fine man outside again. I might have to invite him to *my* place and show him how a real woman is supposed to treat him."

Meghan pressed her lips tight and sucked in a deep breath.

Rory smiled, but his focus was a little off as he glanced over his shoulder at her front door. He texted someone then looked up to face the two women before saying, "I don't doubt you could try," Rory said. "But I'll put my money on Meghan every time."

*Well damn. Points to Mr. Tannous.*

* * *

Rory slid out from behind the wheel, walked over to the passenger side, opened her door, then grabbed her bag and tossed it over his shoulder.

Meghan scanned the pathway and grounds leading up to Rory's mansion. The drive in was nothing short of spectacular, but as they crossed the threshold of a set of ornate double doors she entered a world that reflected understated opulence.

Gray veined, white marble pillars flanked each entrance at the sides of the circular foyer. A small-scale replica of the fountain out front was surrounded by white vases filled with blush roses. Golden framed art with Arabic symbols and script had a home on the wall between a double spiral staircase. The space was warm despite having wall to wall white granite Kashmir tile.

Meghan stopped and slowly spun around just taking it all in. She'd been in the homes of lawyers and politicians before, but she'd never seen anything quite like this.

Rory observed Meghan as she touched the framed art, then inhaled the scent of the flowers. He smiled as her face radiated pure pleasure. He leaned against a pillar with his arms crossed over his chest and waited while she took a spin like a ballerina. Meghan looked right in his home, like she'd already lived there forever.

"Please, come this way." Rory took Meghan's hand and guided her through the dining room, down a hall to the room that would be her home for the next few days.

"I can't believe this is your place. I can't believe this is anyone's home," Meghan laughed as she sat on the plush California king sized bed. "My little spot could fit into this camp twelve times over."

"I'm happy you're comfortable," he said, placing her bag near the white mirrored armoire in the corner of the room. "My mother is a decorator. She's American, born here in Alabama. One of the good things she brought back from the Middle East was the beauty of the culture."

Meghan tilted her head as she watched Rory's lips move with each word he spoke but wasn't focused on anything he was actually saying.

*Don't fall for this man. Don't fall for this man.*

"Do you like your room?" Rory asked as he glanced around, interrupting her self-talk.

"It's gorgeous," Meghan declared, draping a hand over the white Egyptian cotton comforter. "I'd never think to paint my walls turquoise. It's very calming."

Meghan walked to the sliding glass doors leading to a pond and lush garden. "I really appreciate you doing this for me."

"It's my pleasure to accommodate … and keep you safe," Rory replied, his gentle tenor just above a hushed whisper. "With so many people already living here, I don't receive many guests."

Meghan turned on her heels, reclaimed her spot on the bed, pulled the cell from her pocket, and checked the time. Rory glanced at his watch and let out a sigh.

*10:05pm*

"I should get to the party and see what dirt Luis has his hands in," Rory announced, reaching to put her bags down on a nearby padded bench.

"Indeed," Meghan agreed, taking off her shoes and rubbing her feet. "I already know it won't be good. Be careful."

"I will. Make yourself at home. I slipped my contact information in the side pocket of your duffle bag. If you need anything, call me. I'll be back as soon as I can get away."

"Yes sir. I have a date with that gorgeous looking tub in there." Meghan placed her back against the tufted headboard fiddling with the diamond studs Rory had given her.

"I guess I should return these," she said.

"No, they look beautiful on you. Keep them."

She left the bed and crossed the distance between them. "Why do I feel like there's supposed to be a kiss involved when sending you off into danger?"

"Because the fair lady normally does, before her Knight goes into battle," he said, bringing her into his arms. "Or she gives him her scarf."

"I'm all out of scarves," she whispered and placed a kiss on his cheek, closing her eyes as she inhaled the wonderful scent of him.

As she inched away, her gaze lowered to his lips as if they had their own gravitational pull. Giving in, she pressed her lips to his, and for a moment nothing existed in her world but them.

Rory's intense gaze locked on her and in the blink of an eye he claimed her mouth again with his own. She opened to him, and he tasted her, teased her, pulling her against him. That kiss. That damning kiss exploded into a world of sensual exploration that made her knees nearly give out. Only his strong hold kept her from sinking to the floor.

If he was that amazing with a kiss … "Mi dios," she whispered, causing him to give a low, throaty chuckle.

"You speak Spanish?"

"I think that's about all I know," she whispered.

"See, I have you calling on God and whatnot," he teased. "Must be doing something right."

Meghan tossed her head back and laughed.

Rory stroked his fingers down her face. "There's a lot of promise in your kisses, Meghan."

"Difference is," she said with a lot more confidence than she actually felt. "I think I can deliver."

Rory claimed her mouth once more and pulled away. "We keep this up and nothing else will get done." He inched back towards the door. "I'll be back."

"Is that a promise or a threat?" she asked, placing her hand against his chest.

"A little of both." Rory embraced her. "Meghan, I know you want to be hands-on with this, but I need you to stay put. I won't be able to concentrate if I don't know that you're here, safe in my home. Understand?"

"All right," she conceded, then went over to her bag and pulled out something to drape around his neck. "But you keep me posted, the first moment you can."

"I got you," he said, looking down at what she had placed on him. "A sock, Meghan?"

"I told you, I'm all out scarves," she said. "But there'll be more kisses later."

"Is that a promise or a threat," he asked, inching backward, keeping her in his line of sight until he had no choice but to turn and walk down the hallway.

She waited until his footsteps faded to nothing before she fell back on the bed and stretched out, smiling and sending up a prayer for the safety of everyone involved.

*I need you to stay put. I won't be able to concentrate if I don't know that you're here, safe in my home.*

"Good evening," a woman's voice said from the threshold.

Meghan looked up to see a beautiful woman with creamy skin, long black hair, and a soft smile, holding a set of plush towels.

"May I come in?" she asked in a demure voice.

Meghan sat up. "Sure, I'm Meghan."

"I am Chrissy," she said. "Rory's mother."

"Oh, I didn't…"

"No worries," she said with a smile. "I was really being nosy. Rory has never brought anyone home unless they're family. And definitely not a woman."

"Well, it's nothing like that," Meghan protested.

"I came in on the tail end of that kiss," she said with a smile. "It's everything like that."

With that, the woman draped the towels on the tufted velvet chaise lounge and left as quietly as she came.

*It's everything like that.*

Moments later, Meghan took one more glimpse at her cell, a notification banner lit up the screen that she'd missed a call from Mama Ann.

*What could Mama want at this time of night—*

Meghan tapped the screen, returning the call. "Hey Ma—"

"Where are you, Meghan?" Mama Ann screeched, her voice shaking.

Meghan shot up from the bed.

"Them white boys done shot Theresa, and they got the Chief."

"Mama no," Meghan yelled into the phone as she scrambled to collect her bag.

"They said meet them at Tutwiler Prison in an hour, or they're gonna make sure no one finds their bodies."

For a split second she thought of reaching out to Rory, but there wasn't time. He had one set of problems to solve, and this was hers alone.

*Sylacauga is a ninety-minute drive. How the hell do they expect me to make it in an hour?*

# Chapter 29

Rory ran up to his room, grabbed his passport, and rushed down the stairs and found Malakai sitting at the dining table with a bottle of tequila and two shot glasses.

"I see you have company," Malakai taunted, tipping the bottle over one glass.

Rory ran a hand through his hair, frustrated that his brother would show up now of all times.

"How is that any of your business, little brother?" Rory inquired, noticing Malakai was dressed far too fancy to be drinking alone in the formal dining area.

"I can't say for sure that she *is* my business … yet," Malakai replied with a cocky grin.

Rory inhaled and let it out slowly, an attempt to calm his mounting frustration.

"Where are you going all dressed up?"

"With you. Luis invited me too. I was going to drive, but since you're here—" Malakai smirked as he got up and drained the last of his drink.

Rory twisted his lips in disgust, glaring at his brother who had started the party much too early. Something was going on with him. The unhealthy and unexpected anger towards their mother was new and unexplained. Partying was the only thing he was interested in recently, and he seemed to time his infrequent visits for anytime Rory was out of the house. For as happy as he seemed when he picked Rory up from the airport, things went south pretty quick.

"Let's go."

*How is my brother connected to Luis? He can't be involved in this mess with Futtaim.*

"Siri, Cirano's Palace," Malakai said as he dropped into the passenger seat. Rory slid behind the steering column and zipped away from the estate. Malakai evaded every question Rory had regarding his whereabouts, and his flat sullen responses gave no clue as to his state of mind.

"How did you make it home so fast," Rory questioned, narrowing his gaze as if Malakai were sitting in the windshield.

"What do you mean?"

"Weren't you at the gala event? I know my brother's voice when I hear it. When did you leave?"

A wicked smile spread across Malakai's face, but he said nothing.

When they made it to Oxmoor Road, Rory pulled over and texted James, asking if there had been any strange experiences with Malakai.

The answer was slightly alarming.

*He's been trying for days to get your mother to leave the estate, but she refused every time. Even she could feel that something wasn't quite right about him and what he was asking. She doesn't go anywhere except with my wife or Marcus' wife.*

Rory arrived at a building situated on Eleventh Avenue North, pulled into the underground garage, rolled down the window and allowed the guard to scan the barcode from the invitation on his phone. He parked the car and walked toward the entrance, a marked metallic bronze door several feet ahead of him.

"You okay, big brother?" Malakai peered at Rory, clasping his hand on his shoulder before walking in.

"I'm fine," Rory responded, shrugging Malakai's hand off. "I just want to get this over with."

"Well, don't worry about me. It seems I have some new family connections to reestablish." Malakai rushed through the doors while Rory kept his distance by making sure to stay a few paces behind.

The aroma of Bergamot cigars hit Rory as he entered the dark, smoky room, lit only by candles and dim red lights. Further in, red tufted chairs around small ornate gold tables complete with hookahs decorated the space. Gold poles and cages reserved for the entertainment, were staged throughout the vast room and scantily dressed women danced inside.

Rory scanned the cages, looking for women who fit the descriptions he'd been given.

Malakai wandered off to the bar to get drinks as Rory continued taking in the whole scene. Red velvet curtains sectioned off small areas of seating, most were partially drawn. Moaning sounds reverberated from different places in the room, assaulting Rory's ears. His jaws tightened which made for a fast-developing throb at his temple.

Rory's gaze darted around corners and along the walls as he continued to walk through the hazy space. Teary eyes, furrowed eyebrows, and bruised faces followed Rory wherever he stepped. Memories of his mother's abuse flashed before him as he passed women who were crouched in corners, waiting. He approached a back-corner space where Maria was seated outside of a private room, listening, her face streaked with tears, as Luis kept going toward his climax.

Futtaim sat across the space with a cigar in his mouth, his focus on a girl who looked no older than sixteen, dancing for him as he watched. Rory closed his eyes against the anger that threatened to surface. This scene was all too familiar...

"Rory, you made it," Luis shouted as he emerged from the make-shift room. "Welcome!"

Rory tried not to let his face register disgust as a bare-chested woman stumbled from behind the curtain.

"Miss, are you okay?" Rory asked, trying to keep the woman—the girl—from falling.

"Hell yeah, she's okay," Luis answered, irritation coloring his voice. "She's getting good money to play with us tonight." He spread out his hands, gesturing to mean everything surrounding them. "You want some? Sit down, I'll have a sharmuta go get you one of your own. You just have to make a donation, of course."

Rory adjusted his collar to release the heat that built up around his neck, resisting the urge to plant his fist in Luis's face.

Luis laughed as Futtaim looked on. "Oh, I forgot. Mr. Tannous won't take a girl. He's much too righteous for that, isn't that right?"

Futtaim stood and held out his hand for Rory to shake.

Rory stared at the hand and didn't make a move to accept it.

"This disrespect will cost you," Futtaim growled, his dark brown eyes flashed with fire.

Rory nodded, but didn't reply as his steely gaze panned to Maria, whose weakened appearance gave him pause.

"Are you all right?" he asked, holding her gaze for a moment.

She nodded but withered under Futtaim's hard glare and didn't say anything.

"Where's your date, Rory?" Luis taunted glancing over his shoulder. "You didn't bring Miss Turner with you for the fun?"

Rory shot a glare at Luis, and Maria flinched at the mention of Meghan's name. "I only met Miss Turner this evening, remember? I was assigned to the same table that she was. I brought my brother Malakai, which you would know since you invited him."

"Malakai is a great guy," Luis crowed. "He's a regular. Has *special* taste."

"Then why were you so insistent on *my* attendance tonight? Malakai is his own man."

Luis smirked as he looked over at Futtaim.

"I requested your presence tonight, Mr. Tannous," Futtaim stated, taking puffs from his cigar between every few words. "I heard you were back in Birmingham for a while, and I thought this might be a good time to continue our last conversation." He shifted, and his girth seemed to fill up the small red sofa he was spread out on. "You left the meeting so abruptly, and I never heard back from you." He gestured to the empty seat near him. "Please. I have sent for Malakai to bring your drink to my private area."

Rory took a seat but kept his focus outward on everything going on in the room. He made a mental note not to drink anything that came from his brother's hand.

Malakai arrived and handed a glass to Rory before setting his down on the table beside the hookah. "It's good to see you, Baba."

"Son, have a seat," Futtaim said with a grin of his own. "Let's bring your brother up to speed, yes?"

A devious smile spread across Malakai's face as Futtaim presented him to Rory as though he was a stranger. "Malakai and I will be working together. He is responsible for all of the beautiful women you see here tonight."

Rory tried to keep his expression neutral, though the information felt like a punch to the gut.

"He has told us all about your shelter in Durabia that you were so reluctant to share with me at our meeting in Nadaum last year. It's a shame too, as I would have been so honored to fund this little project of yours."

Rory didn't utter a word as he worked to keep his composure as Futtaim continued.

"Malakai has been working with Wellbound and was a big part of getting Luis on the board. Did you know that your brother shares the same passion as you for *saving* women? Well, not all of them. *His* kind of *saving* is reserved for a special woman."

Rory glared at Malakai who was sitting back with his legs crossed comfortably, donning a devilish grin. "Brother, why the look? You told me to find a way to support myself, and I did. All of the money you have, and you wanted me to work. I wasn't cut out for rehabbing houses. The flesh trade is an industry that is as old as time itself."

"You must not know what this man did to our mother," Rory stood, pointing in Futtaim's direction. "He raped her, Malakai. Since it seems he has revealed his true identity to you. That is how he became your father."

His brother didn't even blink or move one muscle as his wicked smile grew. "Mama just couldn't appreciate what Baba gave her. We've been making up for lost time."

Malakai enthusiastically explained his role to Rory, who barely recognized his brother.

"While you were playing god, I've been working behind the scenes to build my own empire. I screen the women who come to Wellbound for help, and if they meet the criteria, I show them a *better* lifestyle. They get clean from their addictions and diseases, and I put them up in my house to live a life of luxury while serving visiting dignitaries of Birmingham in a special kind of way. I've never heard a complaint out of them."

Rory couldn't believe any of this was happening. "Listen," he snapped, grabbing Malakai by the collar and shoving him back in his seat. "I want no part of what you're doing with *your* father."

"I think you will," Futtaim assured, taking a drag of his cigar. "I know all about your little shelter for sad housewives who want out of their marriage. I hear you have my sister-in-law in there. Keep that one. My brother is better off without her. However, Miss Turner is on her way as we are speaking."

Rory released his brother who slid to the floor as Rory whipped around to face Futtaim. "What are you talking about?"

"The Bradland Boys and I have one interest in common—Meghan" Luis informed him. "They don't like her interfering in their business. Neither do I. Her good deeds are cutting into their profits when her clients don't end up back on the streets when they're released. Or that their wives and girlfriends run to her whenever the men have to put them in check."

"So in exchange for Miss Turner's safe return, you must do one thing."

"What's that?" Rory asked, breathing slow measured breaths to calm himself down. Threats from other men didn't usually bother him, but he was unnerved that Futtaim thought to involve Meghan.

"You must return your mother to me."

Rory's heart stopped; his stomach twisted in knots. His mother had experienced hell with Futtaim whenever his father was away on business. Sharia law gave him the confidence to treat his mother the way he did.

When she escaped with all of her children and the clothes on her back, she vowed never to return to Nadaum or reveal the truth to Malakai about his real father. She only told Rory about Futtaim before they left Nadaum, just in case something happened to her. Now he was left to figure out how to deal with Futtaim so he didn't hurt Meghan or his mother.

"You must bring her to me and surrender your shelter in Durabia and the ones in Iran and Nadaum as punishment for the women you have stolen from me."

Rory's temples flexed with each arrogant demand from Futtaim.

"Absolutely no fucking way am I going to have any part in this business. My mother doesn't belong to you or with you. Meghan had better not be harmed or my disrespect is the last thing you'll be concerned about," Rory said calmly with a neutral expression in order not to reveal the anger and fear he was feeling over the danger the two women in his life might be in.

Futtaim leveled a steely gaze on Rory. "That is where you are wrong," he warned, his nostrils flaring above his dark moustache. "Miss Turner will die tonight if you do not let me know your choice by the time she arrives at the prison. She believes she's been called there to rescue her Mama and Chief Carrolton and the five women who are coming with me."

A smile spread across Rory's face as he stood, looking down on Futtaim's short, wide frame. "You underestimate me and my connections, Futtaim. But I'll let you find that out on your own. Good night."

# Chapter 30

Meghan sped down the freeway to Tutwiler Prison, her mind swirling with questions about how Luis was caught up in such an evil scheme with trafficking already imprisoned women.

Pulling onto the raceway outside of the prison, Meghan parked in a far corner of the parking lot, turned off the headlights, and lowered the window. She locked her doors, satisfied the darkened location was the perfect spot for her to watch for transport vehicles coming and going.

"Boss said midnight."

Meghan sank into her seat as she surveyed the nearly empty lot, looking in the direction of the voices.

"You're fifteen minutes late. The guards will be making their rounds again in five minutes. You put the whole thing in jeopardy."

Unsure of where the voices were coming from, Meghan rolled up her windows. She pulled out Rory's card and programmed his number into the SOS contact, hoping she didn't need to call.

Meghan jumped when she heard something hit her car, and the SUV shook. She pulled out her phone and hit the emergency call number and tucked the phone in her bra. She turned her head and squinted at the flashlight shining in her face.

"This is Rory—"

"Roll down your window," said a graveled voice with a Southern drawl.

Meghan glanced behind her, looking for any indication the police were the ones questioning her.

 "No, I think I'm good. I'll be leaving now."

Meghan reached to start her car, but the man on the other side of the glass slammed a pipe into the window.

"I don't think so, bitch, you're comin' with me," the gruff, yet familiar voice growled, yanking Meghan out of the car.

 "Let. Me. Go." Meghan screamed, kicking the man in his shins. "Where's Mama Tee?"

The man dragged Meghan from behind, the stench of rotting teeth and cigarettes making her nauseous.

"Stop screaming, ain't nobody gonna hear you out here," the burly man taunted, losing his breath with the fight. "Them women in that prison scream all fucking night, and nobody hears. We got you."

The man threw Meghan to the ground, her head hitting the gravel before he bent a knee into her sternum. The phone didn't budge from its secured spot.

*Thank God for ample breasts and good bras.*

"This's what you get for makin' The Bradland Boys chase ya out and getting that pig cop involved. Didn't nobody teach ya to act like a proper Southern lady?"

"Shut up," Meghan snapped as she grabbed at the man. "Get off of me. And give me my Mama."

 "Don't worry about ya mammie. She's gonna have 'nuff worry for the both of ya when ya don't make it home tonight," the man said, pushing his knee further into her chest.

Meghan struggled to breathe while she kicked and flailed until the man lifted his knee.

"I might should give her a taste of a real man," said the voice of another man, the sound of a zipper following his declaration. "Fry and old Futt-whatever his name is won't mind."

The mystery men she recognized from the jogging trail laughed as they threw Meghan into the back of a transport vehicle, hitting her head against the frame of the van.

"Jimmy Bob, take her picture and send it to Fry. Tell him we got the bitch. Maybe we'll collect that fifty-grand after all."

Meghan put her hand up to cover her eyes as the flash lit up her face. A sharp pain and cool air sent a chill through her body even though the night was warm. Patting the wet spot on her head, she brought the bloody hand to her face.

"We gotta hurry. The dude's jet takes off at midnight an' we still have to get the girls."

The truck pulled into a service port, where guards were prepared to load the five women on the van.

"We've got a bonus tonight," Jimmy Bob said with an evil grin. "Take her with you where you take the rest of these whores. Get them the hell out of 'Bama."

# Chapter 31

*I've got to get to Meghan.*

"Yes," Luis said as he got up, rushing out of the private curtained area of the party.

Rory turned on his heels to see what had Luis so excited and found him huddled over Futtaim, displaying his phone.

Rory's mind raced as he saw the picture that brought on Futtaim's evil smile.

"Excellent," Futtaim uttered and nodded, his gaze shifting to Rory. "What a perfect night after all. Looks like you have work to do. Tell your mother I cannot wait to see her again." Futtaim stood and turned to Malakai. "Son, get the car. We have an appointment to keep."

Rory looked at Malakai with disgust. "Malakai, do not return to *my* home. I'll deal with you later."

"Brother, I don't understand how you haven't figured it out," Malakai taunted. "I have my own house now. My own properties."

Rory pulled Maria up, and hooked an arm under hers as he steered her through the curtains and across the now crowded club to the front door. Now that business has been concluded Futtaim might kill Maria to tie up loose ends. He had to take her along.

Evidently, Futtaim's plan had been to force Chrissy's return and box

Rory in a corner where he had no choice but to hand over his properties to Futtaim. Not happening. But now Meghan was in his clutches.

Rory settled Maria into his passenger seat, slid quickly behind the wheel and sped away from the club towards the freeway.

"What do they have of Meghan's that would make her walk into their trap? Rory asked.

"Her Mothers," Maria said weakly. "I heard them talking. They put one in the hospital and shot the Chief." She leaned forward, resting her brow on the dashboard.

"Siri, dial Kaleb Valentine."

"Kaleb speaking."

"Futtaim has Meghan," Rory declared, out of breath, his heart pounding against his chest. "He said I have to bring him my mother in exchange for Meghan's safe return."

"Did you give her the earrings like I asked?"

"Yes."

"Daron is live streaming her audio and tracking her and gaining some clues from that. I'm dealing with the women who were auctioned tonight and getting them to safety."

"Women? Being auctioned?" Rory pressed the accelerator.

"You know the piece of art I purchased? The artist was a teen who'd been missing for over six months. The art piece was a coverup. The Wellbound House and their sponsors need to be removed. Every last one of them have a part in this."

Rory drew in a deep breath. He couldn't stand the thought of Meghan being in danger. In the short amount of time he knew her, he couldn't imagine his life without her.

"I'm going back to the house. I have to tell my mother about Futtaim and Malakai and come up with a plan to keep her safe."

"Your brother?"

"Less of a brother and more like Futtaim's son. I'll talk to my *real* brothers about this later. Right now, I have to get to Meghan and my mother."

Rory disconnected the call before Kaleb could respond.

Pulling up to his gate, Rory punched in the code and zipped onto the driveway.

Maria had remained silent for the rest of the trip. He wanted to have compassion, but because of her, his family and Meghan could be killed.

He dashed into the house as Maria lagged behind, to find James and Izzy playing cards at the dining table.

"Rory, man good to see you. Your friend left. We thought we'd stay up in case she came back before you to let her in the gate."

"This is Maria. Please find her a room in Malakai's quarters. He won't be coming back. If he tries, do not allow him past the gate. I'm changing the code tonight and will text you the new one."

James looked at Rory for only a few seconds before giving an affirming nod.

Izzy got up and took Maria by the arms. "Come on sweetheart, let's get you settled. I'll get some pajamas for you to change into and something to wear in the morning."

Maria was too exhausted and scared to ask any questions, so she went without conflict.

"Talk to me, man," James said, his eyebrows drawn into the middle of his face. "What's wrong? How can I help?"

"I'll let you know, but right now I need to see my mother."

"She's in the game room. Late night bridge game with my mom and some friends. There's money on the table. They might cut ya."

A smile slid across Rory's face, glad his mother was awake, but still unsettled about what he had to tell her.

Laughter poured from the game room as Rory sped to find his mother.

"Mama," he said entering the room, all happy noises coming to a complete halt. "I'm sorry ladies. Mama, I need to talk to you."

"Chrissy, I know you taught your boy better manners than this," said one elderly woman, who was stacking pennies in front of her. "He shouldn't be so handsome *and* rude."

Searching her son's eyes, Chrissy gave him a once-over, concerned etched in her expression.

"Ladies, I'll be back to kick your butts and take the rest of your cash in a minute." Pushing her seat back, Chrissy stood and moved close to him.

Rory took his mother's arm and wrapped it around his as they made their way down the hall. He could still smell Meghan's sweet scent in the guest room, and it made his heart ache, wanting her to be safe.

"Mama, Futtaim is back," Rory stated as he and his mother took a seat on the bed. "He and Malakai are dealing in illegal activity and …"

"What is it, son?" Chrissy asked, narrowing her perceptive, blue gaze on him.

"There's a woman I've just met, Meghan …"

"Yes,?" Chrissy's eyes lit up, "the woman that you kissed earlier?"

"You saw that?"

"Yes, she seems delightful."

Rory shook his head, momentarily taken aback.

"Futtaim said he'd kill her and other women he owns if you don't return to him tonight."

Chrissy's eyes grew wide as she stood and moved toward the balcony, shaking her head.

"I'm only sharing this with you because being honest makes everyone alert and aware." She nodded and placed her hand over his. "You might love him, but you cannot trust Malakai. He is working for his father."

"That bastard. He told me that if I ever tried to leave him, he would kill me. You never take a man's firstborn son from him."

"I can't let you go back," Rory placed a hand over hers. "I'll rip his spine out of his body with my bare hands if he touches you."

"Son, I won't let the young lady's life be in jeopardy for my own selfishness. I'll meet with Anwar."

"No, I think we should put someone else in place. I need some of your clothes, your perfume and —"

A vibration from Rory's pocket; Daron's name flashed across the phone screen.

"Daron," Rory exclaimed. "What did you find out?"

"Kaleb gave me the rundown about Futtaim's plans. Send me a picture of your mother." Rory gave his mother a reassuring smile, "Like minds," he said, relieved that they were all on the same wavelength.

# Chapter 32

Meghan woke up, her head throbbing where a lump had formed near her temple. Reality set in. Squeezing her eyes shut and opening them again to see Futtaim glaring at her from his reclining seat, she hoped to wake up from this nightmare.

"We're on a plane?" Meghan placed a hand over her stomach, feeling that her last meal was ready to make an untimely reappearance. "Why am I here?"

"You will address me as Anwar Futtaim," he explained, his voice devoid of emotion. "We are on my private jet on our way to my home in Nadaum. You are here to make certain that Rory keeps his promise to bring me his mother."

Pain radiated in Meghan's head, her heart sinking with the thought of why he would want Chrissy. And his son? Luis? Are they related? "Do you mean Luis?"

"Luis is very helpful, almost like my own son," Futtaim said with a laugh. "Those men from Bradland owed him a favor, so he helped me bring you here. You must have angered him somehow. He was only too ready to give you to me. But I am talking about Rory's brother, Malakai."

"I just met Rory tonight, so I don't know who Malakai is," Meghan quipped. "How am I supposed to help him keep his promise? He doesn't even know who I am."

"Oh, but he does," Futtaim said, lighting a cigar he pulled from an armrest pocket. "I even know a little about you, Miss Turner. I appreciate how you have been able to help me with my business. Your organization is doing a very good thing."

"The Journey Beyond was never meant to traffic women," Meghan said in an attempt to yell, but quickly became dizzy from the effort. "It was meant to give women a second chance at a better life."

"That is what I like about it," he said with an infuriating grin. "I am offering the women a beautiful life outside of jail. And Rory has been thwarting my efforts for too long."

"This is madness," Meghan argued, "Do you really think Rory would sacrifice his own mother for a woman he's just met?"

"That is something we are about to find out," Futtaim said with a sneer. "Rory knows if he does not agree to my terms and bring his mother to me .... you will die."

*Thirteen hours later.*

"Are you sure this is going to work?" Rory asked while he waited on the tarmac, worried for Meghan's safety if any part of the plan failed.

He'd learned to trust the Kings, and understood from briefings on previous rescues that they were near flawless in rescue operations. But the first mission involving people so close to Rory's heart had him shaken. What if they misjudged the timing? What if they ended up in enemy territory with no way to make things right? What if the people who were pulling things together on the opposite end weren't able to get everything into place on time?

"Daron finally patched in, so we're getting a signal from Meghan," Dro assured, placing his aviator shades on.

"Signal? What signal?"

"From the earrings," Kaleb said.

"But they're just a recording device," Rory protested, flickering a gaze between the two men.

"They're much more than that." Dro put a hand on Rory's shoulder. "We know where she is, and we'll have a line on her at all times."

"So they're a tracking device?" Rory asked, both elated and alarmed at the same time.

"Normally the end user has to activate it on their end," Dro said. "But Daron created a software patch the moment he realized Meghan was taken."

"Meghan has trust issues," Rory confessed. "She's going to kill me if she finds out that I put a tracker on her."

Dro chuckled. "But she'll be alive to kill you. So it'll balance out."

Rory flipped him the bird, and the resulting laughter diffused some of his tension.

"Futtaim's plane will land only a few minutes ahead of us, but he's been informed that your mother is on board and that you're complying with his wishes. The pilot has been instructed to keep circling until we touch down. Meghan is still wearing the earrings, and we're picking up her biorhythms. She's alive."

"Why not let him land and have the Durabian authorities pick them up?"

Dro shared a speaking glance with Kaleb who explained. "Because we set a trap for Durabian Nationals who are the main reason this line of trade exists. We shut down the sex den, El Zalaam, a few months ago, then thwarted a major sex and organ trafficking pipeline several weeks ago. Seems like when we put out one fire, another blazes."

Rory frowned, trying to see how Meghan's presence here played into all of this.

"The demand for American women remains high, but Futtaim is now the one supplying and sending them directly into the homes of those Durabia nationals who can afford them."

"So you used Meghan as bait."

"No, Luis saw a way to save his own ass by serving Meghan up to get to your mother, who found Malakai's attempts to lure her away from the house suspicious."

"Rightfully so," Rory shot back. "But I still don't understand why this couldn't have been taken care of on American soil." Rory swept a gaze across the men. "Something isn't right here."

"By time you let us in on the new developments, Futtaim was already two steps ahead," Kaleb explained. "We had to make other maneuvers to ensure Meghan's safety …" His gaze swept to Khalil who was settled in the backseat of the limousine next to a woman dressed in a niqab, only her piercing blue eyes uncovered. "And … your mother."

"I see. Thank you so much for doing this." Rory turned his head to look at Khalil who placed his hand in Rory's and gave it a reassuring squeeze.

"Futtaim has to be stopped once and for all," Khalil said, the power in his voice matched his stern expression. "He should have never been allowed access to your mother in the first place. He was the one who coordinated the mandatory meeting in Nadaum, forcing Jabir to bring Chrissy to him there instead of back to America."

All of the air escaped Rory's chest as he listened to a side of his mother's story he never knew. He knew Khalil was an integral part of their escape from Nadaum, but never heard the reason why his own father turned on his mother that way. Anger at the man who was the root cause of his mother's pain surfaced, and it took everything within him not to let it cloud his actions.

Dro reached in his pocket and extracted his cell placing it on speaker. "Dro here."

"Everything is set. Futtaim's plane is approaching," Daron's voice reported. "We already sent our people in to clear out his properties once he left his home. And his vehicles will be in place just in time. We just need a few more minutes for them to pull into the private hangar. We also scrambled any signals from the area towers."

Reno came out of the cockpit and said, "It's a go. They're on their way out of Nadaum."

Rory's head snapped to Dro. "Who are you talking about?"

"The pilot's family and extended family," Reno said. "He's the one flying Futtaim's jet. He says the women have been given something that kept them sedated the entire trip. But if they awaken while all of this transpires, it could pose a problem."

Rory released a breath he didn't know he was holding. Knowing Meghan was alive and safe, at least for the moment, put his mind at ease, but only a little since the rest of the plan the Kings laid out was still a mystery to him.

# Chapter 33

Futtaim's white and gold trimmed Escalade arrived on the tarmac. Futtaim stepped out of the vehicle, and Meghan followed wearing the same clothes from the day before. Her head was bandaged underneath that messy, tangled ponytail. She looked like what she'd been through, and Rory had to plant his feet so he wouldn't run to her.

Despite the dark emotions rolling through him, a wide bright smile split Rory's face at the sight of her.

"Looks like there wasn't a meal that man ever missed," Dro said, his signature sarcasm colored his tone as he offered Rory a sideways grin.

"Alejandro Reyes," Khalil chastised as Rory chuckled, and the woman giggled from behind her mask.

Rory swung open the rear passenger door.

Futtaim smiled as the diminutive woman exited the vehicle dressed in all black. "Bring her to me," he demanded.

"You send Meghan first," Rory countered.

Several tense moments ensued. "They meet at the halfway mark," Futtaim commanded.

Meghan stumbled as Futtaim shoved her in the direction of the awaiting caravan.

Rory kissed the veiled woman on the cheek before saying loud enough for Futtaim to hear, "I love you, Mother I don't know how I'll ever repay you."

She nodded and her blue glass-like orbs twinkled before as slipped past Meghan, who sprinted towards Rory.

Rory held his arms wide to embrace Meghan, then helped her quickly into the backseat of the limousine. Khalil swung open his door and stepped onto the tarmac, watching the slow progression as Futtaim's smile widened.

"Chrissy could not believe that she would be out of my reach forever," Futtaim boasted with a laugh as he blew cigar smoke into the air where Khalil stood. "I told you."

"Yes, you did," Khalil admitted, leveling a steely gaze on the robust man. "I have promised her that you would never hurt her again, but she wanted her son to be happy. Do not mistreat her. Honor her, for her son's sake."

"Right now, it is none of your business how I treat my wife." Futtaim threw down his cigar and climbed into the vehicle but before the door closed completely, he said, "Rory, I will call you to conclude the rest of our business arrangement. As long as I have your mother in my possession, you will do what you are commanded."

The driver took off down the tarmac, leaving Khalil and Rory on the blacktop.

Dro pulled up, and Khalil dropped into the front seat as Rory entered the back. Pulling Meghan into his arms, Rory rocked her as she buried her face in the wall of his chest.

"It's All right now," Rory whispered. "You're safe."

"Thank you, but your mother isn't, and I'm here and Candace isn't."

"Don't worry about my mother. She's still at my estate," he said, ignoring her wide eyes and questioning glare as he asked, "Dro, any word Candace Simmons?"

"Call Daron," Dro said into his phone.

"Speak," Daron answered after the second ring.

"Do we have Candace Simmons accounted for?"

"She wasn't in with the group we extracted from Futtaim's palace.

She'd already been sold to Futtaim's cousin. We have a team there ... negotiating her release as we speak."

Meghan covered her mouth as though barely holding herself together. She didn't even have a moment to celebrate her freedom before the anxiety about Candace resurfaced.

Silence stretched for an eternal ten minutes before Kaleb came back with, "She's being transported to Rory's shelter here in Durabia."

Both hands went up to cover Meghan's face as she cried. Rory pulled her into his arms and cradled her, kissing her forehead. His relief at her happiness was so profound he had to close his eyes.

"Thanks, bro." Dro disconnected the call.

Meghan finally pulled away to look at him. "Oh my god," she squealed, embracing Rory once again. "Thank you so much. Thank you so very much."

"It's my pleasure," Rory whispered into her hair. "I'll do whatever I can to make you happy."

* * *

Futtaim's driver sped away as he settled in the rear seat with the woman he planned to make his wife.

"Your eyes are even more beautiful than I remember, my dear," Futtaim said as he lifted a hand to touch her face. She leaned away from his reach.

Heat blew up his neck as he glowered at the woman who dared to defy him, even now that she was back under his power and control. "You move away from me? This is the disrespect you give me after so long away from me?"

Futtaim drew back his hand to swing. The woman snatched off her face covering with one hand and brandished a Beretta M92FS pointed at his chest with the other.

"You are not Chrissy," Futtaim shouted, shaking with rage. "Turn around! We have been tricked."

"No, I'm not," the woman agreed with a smile. "Rory Tannous asked me to send you a message. Your days of abusing women are over."

# Chapter 34

The sounds of music and laughter filtered through the door as Meghan showered and slid the loose-fitting ecru dress over her head. Checking her reflection in the mirror, she rubbed the bruise on her forehead from where she hit her head when the men threw her in the truck.

For a minute, the memory of Rory holding her came to mind and a feeling of warmth and happiness came with it. She closed her eyes, relishing everything he had done since then to ensure she was well taken care of. She wanted for nothing. And though every look he gave her was filled with a smoldering heat, he kept a slight distance, giving her the choice of moving things along at her own pace.

Then another thought came to her mind. Sue Ellyn. At the rate things had happened, it was likely that Meghan would need a new residence by the time she made it back from Durabia. Well, everything would sort itself out.

The ultra-feminine buttercream and rose gold accented suite reminded her of something out of a home decorating magazine. The opulence alone spoke of comfort on a level Meghan could easily get used to. An hour earlier, she had woken in the massive circular bed next to a dozen pink and cream-colored roses held together with a satin ribbon and a note.

'*As you sleep, all I dream of is you. R*'

"Meghan, are you coming out today?" Candace asked, peering into the master bedroom of the suite, her smile beaming across her face. "The celebration started hours ago, and we've been waiting for you. Rory's been waiting."

"I hear y'all, and it's the most glorious sound I've ever heard." Meghan gave her a smile. "I didn't mean to keep you waiting, but I needed that sleep. Rory's waiting, you say?"

"Girl, you better come on," Candace said with a laugh. "I've been ear hustling around him and those Kings. I heard one of them say that Futtaim was dead with one gunshot to his forehead."

"Good," Meghan said, the coolness in her voice almost told the story of her reply. "The world should never have a man so evil walking freely."

"Beyond that, all Rory keeps talking about is seeing your face this morning and those Kings keep teasing him about it," Candace declared with a chuckle. Meghan glanced over her shoulder to see her friend standing with her hand on her hip. "We need to go. It's afternoon already."

"Well, I shall not keep him waiting any longer then." Meghan closed the distance between the bathroom and Candace, who waited by the door. Probably for the millionth time since Candace walked out of the doors of the shelter, Meghan threw open her arms and received her with a tight embrace.

They stayed locked in an embrace forever and yesterday. Rory and the Kings moved forward, creating a circular band of protection around them as they watched. When Meghan pulled away, she gestured to the men.

"This is Rory and his brothers. They helped me find you." Candace extracted herself from Meghan's hold, quirked her right eyebrow and said, "Brothers?"

Kaleb chuckled as he said, "Yeah, we get that a lot." One by one, Candace embraced them, saying, "Thank you." Then she peered over

Rory's shoulder at the several vehicles that had transported everyone to this location.

"Where's Emir?"

The men shared a speaking glance and Candace moved closer to them. "Where. Is. Emir?"

Kaleb placed a hand on her arm, steadying her because her hands were trembling. "We don't know," he said. "He had to go underground because the guards informed Futtaim he was the one to help you escape. We haven't been able to find him."

"No. no. no. no!" she cried, slapping a hand against his chest. "He. He. Oh…" she buried her head into his chest as Meghan came forward to collect her from him.

"You don't understand," Candace cried. "He was the only one who kept me believing there was hope. The others, they said such demeaning things. They wanted to…" She shook her head. "He wouldn't let anyone touch me. He slept outside the door to make sure no one came in at night. He kept his promise. No man has ever done that for me before. He would not let me fall into despair. Kept having me recite whatever inspirational messages I could remember, just to keep me from losing my mind."

She swept a gaze across all of the men. "You all found me all the way in a desert. This little Black girl from Birmingham. You found me. Now find him. He's on the side of right. He's your brother, too."

The first night, Candace had a video call with her mother, aunt, and children. She came to crash at Meghan's suite of the Durabia seaside palace. Meghan hand washed her undies and hung them on the line provided by the servants. Though they offered to launder them, Meghan felt some things needed to stay closer to home. Candace splayed across the bed.

*Candace had told of the ordeal she experienced and of Emir, one of the men who worked with Rory and Khalil's underground network. She told them how she wasn't sure she should trust him, but something about him felt right.*

*The night he handed her off to another man in the network during the middle of her transport to the man who had purchased her, she said a prayer for Emir's safety because she knew that her disappearance would be tracked to him. The other guards were still angling to have her before she was out of their reach for good. Emir had to put a bullet in the more aggressive of the two and swore he would blame it on their attempt to damage the merchandise before she made it to her rightful owner.*

*She never even got the chance to thank him.*

"Enough fussing with your appearance. You got a man now." Candace grabbed Meghan's hand and pulled her out of the room and down the stairs as they laughed like schoolgirls.

"He's not my man," Meghan shot back.

"Yet," Candace countered with the quirk of an eyebrow. "You'd better lay that on him and reel him in. That's one fish that shouldn't be nowhere near the sea."

* * *

Daron and Kaleb played a hand of bid whist with Rory and Dro on the sea view patio that wrapped the entire back expanse of the palace. Daron ended a phone call, then slid a card across the table.

"Daron, bring us up to speed on things," Dro said, as he tossed a jack of hearts on the table. "What's the judge doing with Luis?"

"Well, Luis will be on trial for twenty-five counts of international human trafficking, one count of murder for a woman who died in transit, as well as a count of murder for hire on Meghan. No bail. No bond."

"Damn, sucks to be him," Kaleb said with a chuckle, throwing down a two of hearts. "What's good on those Bradland Boys?"

"One is in jail after his kitchen style meth lab was raided," Daron continued, putting an ace of hearts on the table. "The other died of an overdose."

"I feel bad for Maria," Kaleb declared, taking a sip of his drink. "She ended up in the very place she was trying to get her family out of. It's a shame."

"You know what else is a shame?" Daron questioned. "Malakai hasn't been found. He hasn't been seen since the party."

"Yeah, a shame," Rory said, disgust tinged his reply. "A shame that they couldn't tie him to any of the crimes, considering all of the parties he attended."

"Any word on the chief?" Shaz inquired as he enjoyed a bite of pineapple chicken kabob.

"He's retiring after these last events," Rory interjected, flicking a three of clubs onto the table. "Theresa is resting and healing. They're talking about having a whole southern style celebration when we make it back stateside."

Rory's heart skipped a beat as he looked up from his hand to see Meghan grace the short distance to the entrance.

"My brother, if you're on my team you can't be losing focus just because the woman of your dreams shows up," Dro teased, as Kaleb and Daron laughed at Rory fumbling the play.

"Excuse me gentlemen, you all are always teasing me about getting a life. Well, my life just walked in." Rory handed the rest of his cards to Shaz and made his way across the vintage Kashan and red Bukhara Persian rugs that blanketed the floors, muting his steps. He made an easy detour around a small group of women in a heated discussion about the dinner celebration tonight and passed the outdoor dining space to get to Meghan.

Meghan met him halfway, and he held her tight, lifting her off her feet. He drew Meghan in closer as his heartbeat crashed against his chest, matching the rhythm of hers. He had never felt anything for any woman this strong.

He stopped questioning it when his brothers told him to go with what he felt and stop second guessing the timing, the sequence, or the vibes he was picking up from Meghan. Learning from each of his brothers how they'd found their mates had more of an impact than they realized. They had power, purpose, money and love. Rory realized that he couldn't let his parents' tragic union be the example he lived by. Even Khalil had been with his mate for thirty years.

"I didn't think I could miss a person as much as I've missed you the last few hours," Rory whispered. "I was going to watch you sleep but didn't want to be all creepy."

"You could have joined me." Meghan whispered as she pressed her face against his neck and sighed. Rory buried his face in her shoulder and shuddered inwardly at the prospect of every second without her being an eternity to endure. Breathing her in made it all too real. The electricity of her touch, the small warm circle of her arms made it clear.

Those hours of uncertainty after she'd been captured were pure hell. Every moment his mind was in torment wondering if she was afraid or if she could feel that he was coming for her. That he wouldn't let her down. She was the missing piece that he never realized existed or that he needed. His life had been so focused on his purpose and the memory of his mother's pain that he hadn't left room for anything that resembled love.

Now things were different. If he let Meghan walk out of his life without taking this chance on being with her…

All he had or would ever need was there in his arms, that soul to soul kind of love was here. A lifetime of regrets for what could have been vanished as her feminine heat radiated through his clothing and kissed his soul.

Rory leveled a heated gaze on Meghan, feeling his temperature rise and an erection trying to become front and center the longer she stayed in his embrace. Tingles raced through his body as she nuzzled into his neck, then placed her hand on his chest again.

"Hey, get a room," Kaleb teased, and everyone laughed.

"How about …" Meghan whispered, placing a kiss behind his ear. "You show me how much you missed me, and then I can show you how much I appreciate you."

With a nip of his lips on her ear, her breathing hitched. "I think I'd like that," he replied before turning around and easing through the doorway into the open room. "But first, may I have this dance?" He swayed gently, drawing Meghan into a slow dance. "I swore that if we ever had the chance, we would finish that dance from the balcony that was interrupted."

"There's no music playing."

Rory held her away from him and turned her in a lazy spin before pulling her close once more. He pressed a kiss to the bruise on her forehead then turned his face down against her ear.

"Meghan, you are my music."

An excited squeal from Candace caught their attention. She sprinted towards an unfamiliar man standing not too far from the Kings. She barreled into his arms, nearly knocking him to the ground, and held onto him in a manner that caused Meghan to look up at Rory with a questioning look. "Emir," she said, answering her own unspoken query.

Meghan looked back at the two of them, still locked in their embrace. "Looks like she's ready to show him something, too."

* * *

After a luxurious meal in a small private dining room, Rory took her hand and led her to an upstairs suite in the guest wing of Durabia's seaside palace. They shared so many kisses along the way he thought they'd never get there.

"I think I'm a little overdressed for this occasion," Meghan said with a foxy grin. "Do you think you can help me out of this dress?"

Rory wanted nothing more. Pressing a kiss on her pouty lips, he reached for the hem of her dress, gently lifting it over her head. He laughed upon seeing the neon pink panties like the pair she had worn on the night of the gala. This time, the matching lace bra made her a sight to behold.

"I see you're wearing my favorite color," Rory teased.

"Really?" she asked, wrapping her arms around his neck. "I thought your favorite color was neon green."

"As long as you're wearing it, whatever it is, it's my favorite."

"I'll have to order some more."

Meghan's trilling laughter filled the air.

Picking her up and laying her on the bed, he drank in Meghan's curves and freckles. He softly caressed her body, tracing every one of her perfect lines until he reached the soft, full curve of her breast. Every flick of his tongue was followed by a slow, sucking wet kiss.

Meghan's breath quickened as he focused all of his attention on each swollen nipple through the lacy fabric of her bra. Every touch of his hand on her skin sent electric sensations through their bodies. A moan escaped as she bit her lip.

"Don't bite your lip. I want to hear you." Rory growled before kissing her wet inner thigh. Bracing her thighs against his shoulders, his fingers venturing her soft, wet folds. Each flick grew bolder, deeper until at last he latched on to her sweet gem.

As her hips bucked against his mouth, Rory twisted his head sharply, sealing his mouth on the sweet wetness of her silken core, taking her until she screamed his name and the evidence of her desire spilled over his chin.

* * *

"I never thought love was in my future," Rory confessed. He lifted a smoldering gaze to hers.

"Meghan, something about you—"

She put her finger up to his lips to silence him. "You already showed me with your mouth. Tell me with your body."

Her fingers worked to unbutton the white shirt that was plastered to his skin. Removing it from his shoulders, she slid the material down his arms, baring his chiseled form. Placing her hand on his chest, she enjoyed the fast beating rhythm.

Moving her tender caress down his body, she reached to unbuckle his pants and was greeted by a generous bulge awaiting her touch.

Meghan arched her back as Rory dipped in, pressing another kiss into the curve of her neck. The cool air and his touch made her body shiver with pleasure.

Rory lingered, taking in her scent, her heat, his ministrations leading him to her sweet, flowing nectar. Reaching over to the nearby nightstand, he pulled out a drawer and retrieved a condom. Meghan took the condom, ripped it open, and slid the condom in her mouth sheathing him in both.

Rory eased her onto the bed, and teased and tested her, branding her with his molten hot need. For every half retreat, she answered with a thrust of her own. Each passion-filled stroke caused tears of delight to fall from her eyes, but his lips swept lightly over her cheeks erasing them. With him, this kind of love would hold no pain or fear. With Rory thrusting in and out of the core of her, all that was or would ever be was there, right there, fusing them together.

Heaven and Hell could exchange places, but their love would forever be new. She closed her eyes and tightened her pelvic floor, welcoming the length of him to the secret places within. Meghan wrapped her legs around Rory's chiseled body, rocking and swaying her hips to his smooth and thunderous rhythm. And as she was swept away on a current of emotion with his desire filling her to the brim, the sound of Rory moaning her name gave her the sweetest release.

"I can't go back, Meghan," Rory implored as he remained inside, enjoying the warmth and pulse of her walls. "I can't just be a friend or protector or just a lover. I am all of those things and more. I never want to live another day of my life without you."

Meghan ran a hand through his dark, wet curls, catching her breath, smelling his skin. "You never have to," she assured him.

Don't miss the hot new standalone series. The Knights of the Castle made them family, but the Knights will transform the world.

**Book 1 - King of Durabia – Naleighna Kai**

No good deed goes unpunished, or that's how Ellena Kiley feels after she rescues a child and the former Crown Prince of Durabia offers to marry her.

Kamran learns of a nefarious plot to undermine his position with the Sheikh and jeopardize his ascent to the throne. He's unsure how Ellena, the fiery American seductress, fits into the plan but she's a secret weapon he's unwilling to relinquish.

Ellena is considered a sister by the Kings of the Castle and her connection to Kamran challenges her ideals, her freedoms, and her heart. Plus, loving him makes her a potential target for his enemies. When Ellena is kidnapped, Kamran is forced to bring in the Kings.

In the race against time to rescue his woman and defeat his enemies, the kingdom of Durabia will never be the same.

**Book 2 - Knight of Bronzeville – Naleighna Kai and Stephanie M. Freeman**

Chaz Maharaj thought he could maintain the lie of a perfect marriage for his adoring fans … until he met Amanda. The connection between them should have ended with that unconditional "hall pass" which led to one night of unbridled passion. But once would never satisfy his hunger for a woman who could never be his. When Amanda walked out of his life, it was supposed to be forever. Neither of them could have anticipated fate's plan.

Chaz wants to explore his feelings for Amanda, but Susan has other ideas. Prepared to fight for his budding romance and navigate a plot that's been laid to crush them, an unexpected twist threatens his love and her life. When Amanda's past comes back to haunt them, Chaz enlists the Kings of the Castle to save his newfound love in a daring escape.

**Book 3 - Knight of South Holland – Karen D. Bradley**

He's a brilliant inventor, but he'll decimate anyone who threatens his woman.

When the Kings of the Castle recommend Calvin Atwood, strategic defense inventor, to create a security shield for the kingdom of Durabia, it's the opportunity of a lifetime. The only problem—it's a two-year assignment and he promised his fiancée they would step away from their dangerous lifestyle and start a family.

Security specialist, Mia Jakob, adores Calvin with all her heart, but his last assignment put both of their lives at risk. She understands how important this new role is to the man she loves, but the thought that he may be avoiding commitment does cross her mind.

Calvin was sure he'd made the best decision for his and Mia's future, until enemies of the state target his invention and his woman. Set on a collision course with hidden foes, this Knight will need the help of the Kings to save both his Queen and the Kingdom of Durabia.

**Book 4 - Lady of Jeffrey Manor – J. S. Cole and Naleighna Kai**

He's the kingdom's most eligible bachelor. She's a practical woman on temporary assignment.

When surgical nurse, Blair Swanson, departed the American Midwest for an assignment in the Kingdom of Durabia she had no intention of finding love.

As a member of the royal family, Crown Prince Hassan has a responsibility to the throne. A loveless, arranged marriage is his duty, but the courageous American nurse is his desire.

When a dark secret threatens everything Hassan holds dear, how will he fulfill his royal duty and save the lady who holds his heart?

This is a tale of duty, desire, and danger.

**Book 5 - Knight of Grand Crossing – Hiram Shogun Harris, Naleighna Kai, and Anita L. Roseboro**

Rahm did time for a crime he didn't commit. Now that he's free, taking care of the three women who supported him on a hellish journey is his priority, but old enemies are waiting in the shadows.

Rahm Fosten's dream life as a Knight of the Castle includes Marilyn Spears, who quiets the injustice of his rough past, but in his absence a new foe has infiltrated his family.

Marilyn Spears waited for many years to have someone like Rahm in her life. Now that he's home, an unexpected twist threatens to rip him away again. As much as she loves him, she's not willing to go where this new drama may lead.

Meanwhile, Rahm's gift to his Aunt Alyssa brings her to Durabia, where she catches the attention of wealthy surgeon, Ahmad Maharaj. Her attendance at a private Bliss event puts her under his watchful eye, but also in the crosshairs of the worst kind of enemy. Definitely the wrong timing for the rest of the challenges Rahm is facing.

While Rahm and Marilyn navigate their romance, a deadly threat has him and the Kings of the Castle primed to keep Marilyn, Alyssa, and his family from falling prey to an adversary out for bloody revenge.

**Book 6 - Knight of Paradise Island – J. L. Campbell**

Someone is killing women and the villain's next target strikes too close to the Kingdom of Durabia.

Dorian "Ryan" Bostwick is a protector and he's one of the best in the business. When a King of the Castle assigns him to find his former lover, Aziza, he stumbles upon a deadly underworld operating close to the Durabian border.

Aziza Hampton had just rekindled her love affair with Ryan when a night out with friends ends in her kidnapping. Alone and scared, she must find a way to escape her captor and reunite with her lover.

In a race against time, Ryan and the Kings of the Castle follow ominous clues into the underbelly of a system designed to take advantage of the vulnerable. Failure isn't an option and Ryan will rain down hell on earth to save the woman of his heart.

**Book 7 - Knight of Irondale – J. L Woodson, Naleighna Kai, and Martha Kennerson**

Neesha Carpenter is on the run from a stalker ex-boyfriend.

While fleeing the madness of that relationship, she discovers that Chicago Police sees her as the main suspect in his murder. With everything spinning out of control, she runs into Christian Vidal, a former classmate, who offers her a safe haven in the kingdom of Durabia. Neesha's relief doesn't last long, as her stay in the country causes an international incident and places the royal family at odds with the extradition laws of the American government. Christian is smitten with Neesha's strength, intelligence and beauty, and will do whatever it takes to keep her out of harm's way, including enlisting the help of the Kings of the Castle in America.

As more details surrounding the murder emerge, Christian will have to ask himself … did she pull the trigger?

**Book 8 - Knight of Birmingham – Lori Hays**

As a dedicated advocate for single mothers with tragic pasts, Meghan Turner faces a sinister reality. She uncovers a disturbing pattern of missing mothers who were referred to "special treatment centers" before their release from the Alabama justice system. After reaching out to law enforcement for help, disaster hits close to home when her friend vanishes under those same mysterious circumstances.

While at a political fundraiser, Rory Tannous, overhears Meghan voicing her concerns with what seems to be orchestrated disappearances. The issues speak to his own past when his mother married, then disappeared the moment she and his siblings migrated to a volatile part of the world. He elicited the help of Daron Kincaid, King of Morgan

Park, in his family's rescue and now needs to find Meghan's friend. Along the way, they discover a government alliance of powerful men willing to rid themselves of anyone who stands in their way.

The stakes are high, and discovery may lead to Rory and Meghan's destruction and the disappearance of vulnerable souls.

**Book 9 - Knight of Penn Quarter – Terri Ann Johnson and Michele Sims**

Following a successful FBI sting operation, Agent Mateo Lopez accepts a new assignment that takes him into the world of illegal adoptions between the United States and other nations.

Unfortunately, his love life suffers from the demands of his career. That is, until he meets the classy but "unlucky in love," Rachel Jordan, who has sworn off relationships and commits herself to running a children's social service agency and simpler pleasures. Mateo finds himself falling for her in more ways than one, and when trouble brews in one of Rachel's cases, he does everything in his power to keep her safe and protect the children from danger. Even if it means resorting to extreme measures.

Will the choices they make cost them their lives, or bring them closer together?

*"Did you miss The Kings of the Castle? "They are so expertly crafted and flow so well between each of the books, it's hard to tell each is crafted by a different author. Very well done!"* - Lori H..., Amazon and Goodreads

**Each King book 2-9 is a standalone, NO cliffhangers**

**Book 1 – Kings of the Castle, the introduction to the series and story of King of Wilmette (Vikkas Germaine)**

*USA TODAY*, *New York Times*, and National Bestselling Authors work together to provide you with a world you'll never want to leave. The Castle.

Fate made them brothers, but protecting the Castle, each other, and the women they love, will make them Kings. Their combined efforts to find the current Castle members responsible for the attempt on their mentor's life, is the beginning of dangerous challenges that will alter the path of their lives forever.

These powerful men, unexpectedly brought together by their pasts and current circumstances, will become a force to be reckoned with.

**King of Chatham - Book 2 – London St. Charles**

While Mariano "Reno" DeLuca uses his skills and resources to create safe havens for battered women, a surge in criminal activity within the Chatham area threatens the women's anonymity and security. When Zuri, an exotic Tanzanian Princess, arrives seeking refuge from an arranged marriage and its deadly consequences, Reno is now forced to relocate the women in the shelter, fend off unforeseen enemies of The Castle, and endeavor not to lose his heart to the mysterious woman.

## King of Evanston - Book 3 - J. L. Campbell

Raised as an immigrant, he knows the heartache of family separation firsthand. His personal goals and business ethics collide when a vulnerable woman stands to lose her baby in an underhanded and profitable scheme crafted by powerful, ruthless businessmen and politicians who have nefarious ties to The Castle. Shaz and the Kings of the Castle collaborate to uproot the dark forces intent on changing the balance of power within The Castle and destroying their mentor. National Bestselling Author, J.L. Campbell presents book 3 in the Kings of the Castle Series, featuring Shaz Bostwick.

## King of Devon - Book 4 - Naleighna Kai

When a coma patient becomes pregnant, Jaidev Maharaj's medical facility comes under a government microscope and media scrutiny. In the midst of the investigation, he receives a mysterious call from someone in his past that demands that more of him than he's ever been willing to give and is made aware of a dark family secret that will destroy the people he loves most.

## King of Morgan Park - Book 5 - Karen D. Bradley

Two things threaten to destroy several areas of Daron Kincaid's life—the tracking device he developed to locate victims of sex trafficking and an inherited membership in a mysterious outfit called The Castle. The new developments set the stage to dismantle the relationship with a woman who's been trained to make men weak or put them on the other side of the grave. The secrets Daron keeps from Cameron and his inner circle only complicates an already tumultuous situation caused by an FBI sting that brought down his former enemies. Can Daron take on his enemies, manage his secrets and loyalty to the Castle without permanently losing the woman he loves?

### King of South Shore - Book 6 - MarZé Scott

Award-winning real estate developer, Kaleb Valentine, is known for turning failing communities into thriving havens in the Metro Detroit area. His plans to rebuild his hometown neighborhood are derailed with one phone call that puts Kaleb deep in the middle of an intense criminal investigation led by a detective who has a personal vendetta. Now he will have to deal with the ghosts of his past before they kill him.

### King of Lincoln Park - Book 7 – Martha Kennerson

Grant Khambrel is a sexy, successful architect with big plans to expand his Texas Company. Unfortunately, a dark secret from his past could destroy it all unless he's willing to betray the man responsible for that success, and the woman who becomes the key to his salvation.

### King of Hyde Park - Book 8 -Lisa Dodson

Alejandro "Dro" Reyes has been a "fixer" for as long as he could remember, which makes owning a crisis management company focused on repairing professional reputations the perfect fit. The same could be said of Lola Samuels, who is only vaguely aware of his "true" talents and seems to be oblivious to the growing attraction between them. His company, Vantage Point, is in high demand and business in the Windy City is booming. Until a mysterious call following an attempt on his mentor's life forces him to drop everything and accept a fated position with The Castle. But there's a hidden agenda and unexpected enemy that Alejandro doesn't see coming who threatens his life, his woman, and his throne.

### King of Lawndale - Book 9 - Janice M. Allen

Dwayne Harper's passion is giving disadvantaged boys the tools to transform themselves into successful men. Unfortunately, the minute he steps up to take his place among the men he considers brothers, two things stand in his way: a political office that does not want the competition Dwayne's new education system will bring, and a well-connected former member of The Castle who will use everything in his power—even those who Dwayne mentors—to shut him down.

**Lori Hays** is a debut author with MarZé Scott of Knight of Birmingham. She is a new member of NK's Tribe Called Success which has successfully released three anthologies, and one 9-book series. A loving wife and working mother of two teenagers who spends much of her time on the road listening to books. Other times, you can find her reading, writing, training to become a trail runner, or if she's lucky, painting. Lori has a strong love of creative people and will soon relaunching her podcast *Fantabulous Chats* interviewing people you should know, including fellow sisters and brothers of the pen. Until then, she'll be lost in the pages of her favorite book or jotting down stories for her future readers to indulge in.

www.authorlorihays.com

**MarZé Scott** is the national bestselling author of Gemini Rising and enjoys writing about the twists and turns of life's journey. In collaboration with USA Today and national bestselling authors, MarZé penned King of South Shore, book six in the romantic suspense series Kings of Castle. MarZé is also a contributing author for the NK Literary Café Magazine, as well as the anthologies including Just One Kiss and Sugar.

www.marzescott.com